Nor are they all quite what you might expect, from the mutant faeries of Chernobyl via 'Spirits of Inebriation' (including absinthe, of course) to an interpretation of Redcaps that is quite a divergence from the usual 'murder gnomes.' If you loved *Lady Cottington's Pressed Fairy Book*, you need this on your shelf."

—Jonathan L. Howard,
author of *Johannes Cabal the Necromancer*

"This book resurrected my sense of wonder by providing a lively, luminous look at the possible denizens of Faerie, and it also turned that illumination unflinchingly onto the murkier aspects—such as climate change, and colonization—of our mundane world."

—Freya Markse, fantasy author

"*Finding Faeries* presents a delightful, thoughtful journey through a world far more wondrous than our own. Alexandra Rowland's gently academic prose welcomes us into fantastical whimsy—their post-industrial creations nestle gleefully alongside more traditional cryptids. This haunting and liminal guide, rife with telling details, shows that our era of concrete and climate change can still be home to eldritch wonders—if you know where to look."

—Jennifer Mace,
speculative fiction author and
cohost of the *Be the Serpent* podcast

FINDING
FAERIES

FINDING
FAERIES

DISCOVERING SPRITES, PIXIES, REDCAPS,
and **OTHER FANTASTICAL CREATURES**
in an **URBAN ENVIRONMENT**

ALEXANDRA ROWLAND

TILLER PRESS
New York   London   Toronto   Sydney   New Delhi

TILLER PRESS

An Imprint of Simon & Schuster, Inc.
1230 Avenue of the Americas
New York, NY 10020

First Tiller Press hardcover edition October 2020

TILLER PRESS and colophon are trademarks of Simon & Schuster, Inc.

For information about special discounts for bulk purchases, please contact
Simon & Schuster Special Sales at 1-866-506-1949 or business@simonandschuster.com.

The Simon & Schuster Speakers Bureau can bring authors to your live event.
For more information or to book an event, contact the Simon & Schuster Speakers Bureau
at 1-866-248-3049 or visit our website at www.simonspeakers.com.

Interior design by Jennifer Chung

Illustrations by Miles Äijälä

Manufactured in the United States of America

5 7 9 10 8 6

Library of Congress Cataloging-in-Publication Data

Names: Rowland, Alexandra, author.
Title: Finding faeries : discovering sprites, pixies, redcaps, and other fantastical creatures
in an urban environment / by Alexandra Rowland. | Description: First Tiller Press
hardcover edition. | New York : Tiller Press, 2020. | Includes index. Identifiers: LCCN
2020016761 (print) | LCCN 2020016762 (ebook) | ISBN 9781982150266 (hardcover) |
ISBN 9781982150273 (ebook). Subjects: LCSH: Fairies. | Spirits. Classification: LCC
BF1552 .R69 2020 (print) | LCC BF1552 (ebook) | DDC 398/.45—dc23
LC record available at https://lccn.loc.gov/2020016761
LC ebook record available at https://lccn.loc.gov/2020016762

ISBN 978-1-9821-5026-6
ISBN 978-1-9821-5027-3 (ebook)

Contents

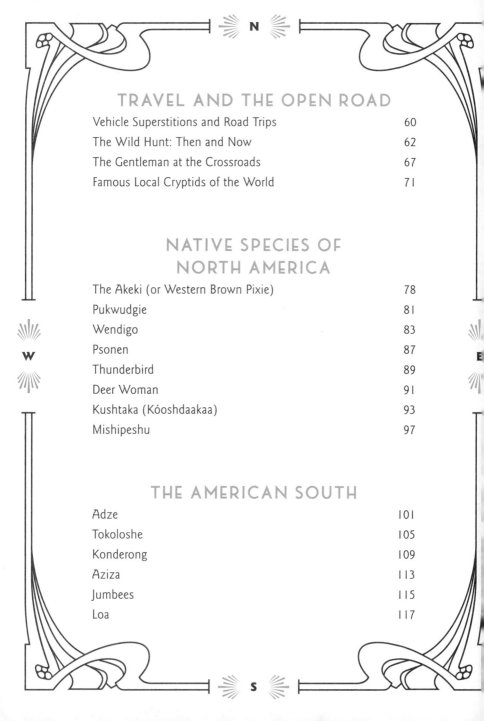

TRAVEL AND THE OPEN ROAD

NATIVE SPECIES OF NORTH AMERICA

THE AMERICAN SOUTH

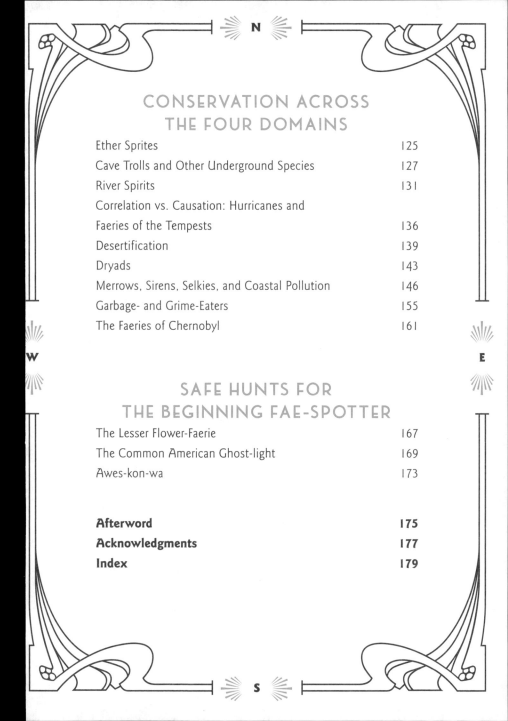

CONSERVATION ACROSS
THE FOUR DOMAINS

SAFE HUNTS FOR
THE BEGINNING FAE-SPOTTER

Introduction

From 1901 to 1957, a crossroads demon occupied Ellis Island, the conjunction of thousands of roads for hundreds of thousands of tired, desperate people. The demon's presence is significant for a number of reasons.

First, of course, because this crossroads demon was one of the earliest documented supernatural beings in the urban American environment. Second, because it encapsulates the way fae and other beings of the liminal world have been forced to adapt to the modern era, just as coyotes, raccoons, pigeons, and other urban creatures have. With the advent of the truly metropolitan age at the beginning of the eighteenth century, important crossroads have proliferated in very condensed spaces, leading to smaller territories for their guardian spirits and an overall weakening of their strength and power.

The changes in the rhythm and arrangement of human life have not been the only factor impacting the supernatural ecology—beings that were once extraordinarily rare have found niches in which to thrive in abundance, while formerly commonplace native species have been driven out by urban sprawl, technological advancements, climate change, and especially by their invasive counterparts. (This is not only a concerning issue for environmentally minded fae-spotters, but also a grim parallel of the historical patterns of human history.)

This encyclopedia covers merely a brief survey of some of the ways the activity of human civilization has influenced these creatures. Rather than discussing the supernatural creatures of the untouched wilderness or rural areas (which have already been exhaustively documented by others), we will instead focus on these urban and suburban environments and the creatures that have adapted to them. With all creatures of the liminal world, especially those associated with the darker and more terrifying aspects of life (such as the redcaps of Europe, which thrive in places where great and monstrous violence has been done), it is worth asking ourselves these questions: Are they causing these horrors? Are they a side effect of them? Do they *make* us do harm, or are they created in the moment when we give in to those impulses of our own will?

Or are the darker aspects of the fae merely a gruesome mirror of the darkest parts of ourselves, external evidence of the internal capability—which all of us carry—to be truly monstrous?

In the modern day, a crossroads demon is far more likely to appear as a tired, tattered vagrant rather than the elegant-suited gentlemen of folktales. However, regardless of their relative power, the old rules for dealing with fae endure: Treat them kindly, speak to them with care and respect, promise them nothing you are not willing to give freely and wholeheartedly, and be careful what you wish for.

On Faerie

When the rigorous and academic study of the liminal world was first being established in the early 1700s, European scholars (most of them white, male, well-to-do, and of a literary persuasion) referred to their field as "the study of Faerie," meaning the study of the *land* where faeries come from. The term "liminal world" did not emerge until the early 1900s, when newer generations of scholars, feeling their work to be less literary and more scientific, began to aspire toward receiving the same sort of respect and adulation from the general public as did their counterparts in physics, engineering, and chemistry. "The liminal world" was therefore adopted as the prevailing term because it sounded more scholarly and less whimsical: "liminal," from the Latin root for "threshold," refers to the in-betweenness of many supernatural creatures and beings. It is not quite of our world, and neither quite outside it: the threshold world; the world of twilight, neither day nor night; the world of the moment between sleeping and waking; the world of no particular color.

More prosaically, and as a fortunate side effect, the change in terminology also opened up the field to contributions from cultures whose local supernatural ecologies were definitively *not* within the Northwestern European model, no matter how many similarities and parallels there are across the world. These contributions have enriched the field immeasurably and have proven priceless in deepening our understanding and knowledge of something that, by its very nature, may never be fully understood or known.

The term "faerie" is complicated for another reason. Though the term for the field of study has changed, "faerie" or "fae" is often still used as a catchall sort of term for beings of the liminal world. With many species, it seems natural to categorize them under the umbrella of "faerie." With others, it seems unsettling or outright wrong. Is a cave troll a faerie? What about a mer-creature?

In a field of study that itself, by its very nature, exists in a liminal space and is supported primarily by amateurs and hobbyists, one must only expect these sorts of disputes over terminology to be commonplace. There is no established foundation of knowledge, no canonized system of nomenclature. Scholars have not even agreed on whether it is appropriate to continue using Latin when structuring a taxonomy of species, due to the possibility of reinforcing Western (and specifically European) bias on a vibrant, worldwide field that we have only just begun to study in any kind of meaningful, formalized way. And yet, at least when speaking English, we nevertheless say "faeries," though we mean a thousand different things.

In this book, when using the word "faeries," I will generally use it to mean liminal creatures that are tied in some way to people or civilization—the humanoid sprites, pixies, and brownies with recognizable human-like faces, two arms, two legs, fingers, and toes, for example. These are creatures that exist as a distortion and reflection of aspects of human nature, as opposed to those connected to the elements (trolls, tommyknockers, kelpies, merrows, etc.). However, across the categories, there are certain commonalities—no matter what kind of liminal creature one is facing, there are good rules of thumb to use or be mindful of, and some of the parallels of similarity between species approach being universal law.

The Movements of the Fae

In the study of the liminal world, it is particularly useful to talk about faeries, specifically—those beings tied in some way to human civilization—because of their patterns of proliferation across the globe: We carry them with us. We have documented hundreds of native species of faeries in North America, and there are hundreds more that have been attested in Native and indigenous folklore. Just as European colonists brought with them invasive species of plants and animals, so, too, did they bring invasive species of faeries, which had just as much of an impact on the local supernatural ecology as their mundane counterparts. The American biologist Anne Lennet, in a letter to her cousin Bartholomew in 1801, wrote:

In years past there were a great many little pixies flying about the lower field near the creek. Clouds and swarms of them! I used to think they were as common as gnats or mosquitoes, but prettier, as bright as bluebottle flies. I have always meant to make a study of them, but you know how these things go, always one important thing after another taking up my attention, and leaving little time for those pleasant small diversions of personal interest. [. . .] This summer, being particularly hot, and following such a difficult winter, I've noticed that there are

many fewer of them, and I have had no luck at all in catching any for sketching.

If Lennet ever had an opportunity to sketch her fae sightings in the first place, then none of those sketches have survived. Scholars estimate that these "bluebottle pixies" must have gone extinct sometime in the decade following Lennet's letter, either due to a more aggressive predatory species or to the human colonists' destruction of their habitats.

When moving on their own initiative, faeries tend to travel along ley lines and congregate near places of power. These may be wells or springs, veins of ore, old forests, grain silos, particularly popular nightclubs, mass graves, or electric and nuclear plants (see "The Faeries of Chernobyl" on page 161). While many faeries consume mundane food, all of them rely on access to sources of power for their life energy. A captive faerie taken into a dead zone will quickly show signs of exhaustion and malaise, followed within a few days by death, where their physical form, if any, will dissolve into dust, sand, or dry leaves.

LEY LINES

In the same way that birds can sense the Earth's magnetic field and use it to orient themselves during their seasonal migration, liminal beings can sense the subtle flows of energy that connect places of power like a worldwide railroad network. Some ley lines are stronger than others, even if they are not connecting two strong power wells. Experienced practitioners can sense ley lines by dowsing (see "Dowsing for Dunces" on page 8), but there are now several popular smartphone apps that make dowsing accessible even to beginners, though most of them are inaccurate and unreliable for finding the smaller, weaker lines. Unless you only require the location of a medium- or high-strength line for a handful or fewer occasions, experts still recommend practicing dowsing by hand with a Y-branch or pendulum. Basic proficiency takes longer to achieve, but it will be far more useful in the long run (and doesn't rely on a fully charged phone battery).

DEAD ZONES

There are, scattered across the world, pockets of stagnation where little or no ley energy flows. Without exception, these areas are fatal to creatures of the liminal world. In some dead zones, a lesser fae (such as a pixie or an air sprite) may die within minutes, whereas more powerful beings can survive perhaps a day or two. Death Valley is one of the largest natural dead zones in North America, but it is far exceeded in lethality by the Uyuni Salt Flats of Bolivia, where even higher-order creatures die within hours.

There are man-made zones, too—most commonly, they are found in the monocrop fields of enormous corporate megafarms, where toxic pesticides, a lack of biodiversity, genetically sterilized crops, and over-tired soil all contribute to a withering of liminal energies. Fortunately, these dead zones can be reclaimed with relative ease over the course of several years by seeding the soil with native trees and plants, especially wildflowers and other pollinator species that support the local insect populations. If this is unfeasible, standard methods of crop rotation can help mitigate the effects of the dead zone somewhat.

DOWSING FOR DUNCES

Dowsing is a method of finding underground water and ley lines that has been practiced since ancient times. The practitioner takes a Y-shaped branch (birch and ash are quite good for this) and holds the forked end, extending the point before them and walking back and forth across an area until the branch points at the ground or tugs in an odd direction. A pendulum on a long string can also be used. Either way, it requires a great deal of patience, care, and sensitivity, but an experienced dowser can make their tools out of odds and ends and never be caught without. Be mindful of dowsing in areas where there may be underground pipes, sewer lines, or electrical cables, as these can give strong disruptive signals.

The Land of Faerie

The liminal world is a place between places. It appears in folklore as a castle that a lost traveler stumbles upon in the middle of the woods, or as a system of glittering caves, or as a forest hall, or as a magical world under the hill. In Faerie, we are told, everyone is beautiful and well dressed and merry, and there is constant music and dancing, feasting and drinking, and it is very easy to become bewitched and forget that time is passing. Humans are warned not to step inside a ring of mushrooms, or to look too closely at the moon reflected on still water, or to wander too deep into the forest. Faerie does not exist at a specific physical location in our world; rather it lies *alongside* our world, offset by a few inches and turned slightly askew. That said, there are certain factors that can bring us a little closer to the hidden world. Much of historical scholarship on this subject has been devoted to determining how to access Faerie (more on this later), but the most successful ventures have usually been accidental. Scholars have wasted an enormous amount of time determining how they could calculate liminality, as if it were something that could be scientifically defined, despite their knowledge that the very heart of liminality is that it cannot be defined; it's as if they tried to be clothed and unclothed at the same time, or fed and unfed, or wealthy and poor, or upside down and right-side up, or wet and dry, or cold and warm—all of these through a series of ordeals and mental acrobatics that seems outright ridiculous to the modern eye. It is not nearly so much about the *seeker* as it is about the place that is sought. In the modern world, one of the most liminal of spaces is the truck stop. It is, as above, a place between places, rather than a place in and of itself. Travelers stop there briefly, move on, and usually *forget* about it, or at the very least their memories blur to indistinctness. Subway cars, too, are strongly liminal spaces, as are bridges, tunnels, hallways, doctors' waiting rooms, and service queues. (Particularly, for some reason, at the post office and bank teller. No one knows why, but also everyone knows exactly why.)

I hesitate to tell you any of this, of course—only the reckless and the very stupid or the *very* experienced attempt to go to Faerie, and I fear that by telling you how, I might encourage you to try before you are ready. Part of the journey of becoming an expert is, after all, the quest for information.

Abbot Edwin of Locksley wrote the earliest account of Faerie that seems to show evidence of being more than just the drunken ramblings of a very bored creative mind. In 1127, he wrote a letter to his local duke:

Your Grace, Tuesday last I was on the road to visit you, and as it was good weather I was walking by foot and decided to cut through the wood, as my eager heart was too impatient to see you. [. . .] I think you may have a band of merry poachers in your wood, my dear, wearing bright colors and playing such music as I have never heard so that my feet itched to join them. Indeed, they called out to me and seemed very pleasant and friendly, but I only replied, "I cannot stop, I am expected at the Duke's table!" It was only the thought of my destination that hurried me onwards, otherwise I expect I would have tarried an

hour or so. Yet when I emerged from the wood, I found myself practically on the abbey's doorstep, just at twilight, though it had been early morning when I set out. I weep to think that you may have waited for me so long without hearing word from me. Be at ease, beloved, I will come to you again on Monday, and I shan't cut through the woods.

Another notable text includes the diary of obscure American essayist L. C. Parsons (who died sometime in the late 1870s), who had apparently visited Faerie several times until the construction of a railroad cut through the copse they commonly used to access it, permanently destroying whatever doorway had been there.

I could not in good conscience give you exact directions for entering Faerie, even if it were possible to do so. Every doorway is a little different. However, the following doorways are all defunct, so they are safe to list, and you may glean from them what clues you can manage to deduce:

1. Los Angeles: Griffith Park, near the
   abandoned zoo.
   FIRST DOCUMENTED: 1922
   WENT DEFUNCT: 1975
   NOTES: Accessible four days after the full
   moon, starting ninety minutes before the moon
   reaches its zenith and lasting ninety minutes
   afterward. Signs included the sound of
   distant laughter and wind instruments. Bring
   a loaf of very good bread.

2. New York City: Central Park, the stand
of trees by the pond behind the Delacorte
Theater.
FIRST DOCUMENTED: 1985
WENT DEFUNCT: 1994
NOTES: Accessible for thirty minutes at
dawn on the equinoxes. Extremely difficult
to locate; signs included rustling of leaves
when there was no wind, or a faint meowing.
Impossible to pass through if the traveler
was wearing shoes with laces or the color
gray.

3. London: Elizabeth Tower (Big Ben), the panes
of glass that make up the numeral VIII on the
eastern clock face.
FIRST DOCUMENTED: January 6, 1878
WENT DEFUNCT: May 10, 1941 (presumed)
NOTES: Opened for one chime of the bell at
midnight every other Thursday, and required
the traveler to be carrying a shilling in
every pocket of their clothing.

GLIMPSES INTO
THE LIMINAL WORLD

One of the most common places and times to catch a glimpse of the liminal world is in the mirages that rise from asphalt in the summer. Interstates, freeways, even common suburban roads—the only trick of seeing is how to bend the eye.

Eyes can be very difficult to bend, though. An infinitesimally small percentage of the population has a slight natural ability (known in folklore as "second sight"). But it is much easier to bend the light itself before it even gets to the eye. Mirages, the shimmering optical illusions caused by heat-refracted light, are well known as a danger to travelers in the desert, where they may walk and walk, thinking that the faint glistening in the distance is water that's always just another mile ahead.

However, more developed mirages show a glimpse beyond even that—not just a phantom oasis, but towers and spires of distant palaces, or great mountain ranges. At sea, sailors have reported sailing toward an island they saw clearly, only to discover that it had vanished. It is probable that at least some of these visions, rather than being mundane mirages, are reflections of the liminal world, which is calculated to exist between 120 and 179 degrees offset widdershins from the mundane. (The leading scholar of this phenomenon, as of the publishing of this book, is Dr. Jenn Lyons, professor of physics and currently unaffiliated with a university.)

The Moral Divisions of Faerie

The popular system of nomenclature for the division of faerie morality is to refer to them as the Seelie (good to neutral) and Unseelie (neutral to evil) Courts. However, this system is Eurocentric, not to mention reductive and without nuance. It constitutes an act of astonishing naiveté to define what counts as "good" or "evil," not only for liminal beings but for the mundane ones as well. Is a wolf evil for killing a human when it is hungry? Are the spirits who feed on fear committing an evil act by inciting it, or are they merely responding to their own evolutionary imperative? (And this even takes the added step of presupposing that Darwinian evolution can even be applied to them.) Evil, one could argue, is about a sentient choice.

Most of the beings discussed so far tend to be described as "morally neutral"—they cause small mischiefs at worst, and most of them have as much impact as a mundane animal. Of the ones who have human-like sentience, the good or ill that they do happens because of *human* choice (consider the Gentleman at the Crossroads, letting his clients choose their own bargains). However, there are also many beings that are actively evil, sometimes so much so that even humans without a sensitivity to liminal energies can feel their presence: for instance, thinking *This feels spooky* about an abandoned house, or getting goose bumps when passing by a cemetery.

When people say "Unseelie," what they generally mean are the sorts of faeries who are actively malicious—those who attack humans for their own amusement and without provocation, for example. The Unseelie, too, cannot be considered "fair" in any sense—they are neither just nor beautiful. The Seelie, by comparison, are regarded as generally benevolent, though this is a profoundly dangerous assumption to espouse. In the community of fae-spotters, it is extraordinarily easy to find individuals arguing that there is no reason to fear a Seelie: "They don't want to mess with you, they're nice, they'll help, they're safe." The Seelie are no safer than the Unseelie, and to call them "nice" is to impose an entirely human system of morality judgment upon them when, in actuality, they exist upon a completely different ethical spectrum. True, a Seelie will probably provide a hint or a warning if you are straying too close to the boundaries of propriety and beginning to offend them, but so do Unseelie—it is only that their warnings are subtler and often nonverbal. (It is a similar situation as when people claim that cats are evil because they will attack "without warning," though the person being attacked has ignored the lashing tail, the flattened ears, and the soft growls.) But regardless of warnings, when we are talking about faerie morality, we never speak about our own actions—and isn't it our own responsibility to behave in a manner that does not offend? Though the faeries have, to our perception, a skewed view of what is Right, their logic is often completely understandable when you see things from their perspective: their property trespassed upon or stolen, their home destroyed, themselves put in danger of losing face. Clear offenses, for which they demand fair recompense.

The actual human-perceived distinction between the Seelie and the Unseelie comes from our own biases and preconceptions: The Unseelie appear (to human judgment) wild and ragged, impoverished, and "uncivilized," while the Seelie look like gracious, wealthy nobility, and that is more than enough to influence human behavior. The Seelie are polite because *we are polite to them*, and the Unseelie are cruel because *we are cruel first*.

BOGGARTS

Boggarts are perhaps the classic example of an evil faerie. A *genius loci* (localized spirit, tied in some way to a particular place), boggarts are universally malevolent. Though some folklore suggests that a boggart is created when a house's brownie becomes enraged from ill treatment, there as yet is no modern documentation of this phenomenon. It is worth pointing out, as a counterargument, that boggarts do not only inhabit houses, but are also found in dens in remote areas such as swamps and bogs, whereas brownies are by nature tied to human settlements. Boggarts, too, are much larger than brownies, oftentimes nearly the size of humans, though they are horrible to look upon— filthy and twisted, with fishy, grayish, baggy skin and tiny eyes. House boggarts are primarily nocturnal and are not obligate timorvores (fear-eaters). They can and do eat small animals when necessary, but human fear nourishes them in a different way (hence our argument that they are *evil*, rather than simply frightening and eerie). If smaller mischiefs do not provoke the reaction they desire, they will escalate. They are known for laying their cold, damp hands on the faces of the house's residents while they sleep and attacking them when they wake. In urban environments they often make dens in old warehouses, boarded-up shops, the backs of dark alleys, or under bridges.

Communicating with the Fae

Traditional folk wisdom holds strong: Don't do it. Don't talk to faeries; don't talk to beings who might be faeries; don't talk to a Gentleman at the Crossroads even if you're desperate, even if he's got a fashionable coat.

Except that it is never as simple as that, is it? Never mind the fact that many of you will think, *Ah, but I am an expert, I know what I am doing.* The fae are, above all, a reflection of human nature, and they go where humans go. They have been carried from continent to continent, as if travelers have hauled them along in back pockets. And where are humans going now?

Mostly, the internet.

To say that faeries "exist" in digital mediums is a gross oversimplification, as well as a fundamental misunderstanding of how faeries "exist" in the world itself. Liminal beings can be a shape of energy, or a vibration in the ether, or an echo. Some can be touched or captured, but many more are as nebulous as ghosts. It is right there in the name: They are called liminal because they are not quite anchored onto this plane, as we are. It is therefore only to be expected that they would follow us even into abstraction, and thus we have faeries of information, faeries of bytes, and pulses of electricity, and magnetic blips.

With this, the maxim of "Don't talk to faeries" becomes suddenly moot, because these days a person might not even know that they *are* talking to one. The maxim must be discussed with greater care, then, rather than intoning a few dire warnings and leaving you to the mercy of your common sense.

As anyone living today recognizes, our social standards of politeness (particularly in North America) have changed and grown more flexible over time; the fae's have not. Those that are capable of human or nearly human communication still require invitations to enter a house, and will become offended if you trespass on their territory. Eating their food is also strongly inadvisable. (This is why you should never eat the food that you find in the cupboards of residences you found through home-sharing services, lest you emerge to find that seven years have passed and you now owe a permanent debt to the faerie of the house.)

The main issue here is bargains. Inviting someone in, or being invited, is a bargain of hospitality; sharing food even more so. As folktales have taught, fae take things quite literally and hold contracts sacred above all else, so even seemingly innocuous statements like, "May I have your name?" become suddenly dreadfully dangerous—except that in the age of social media, most of us are going around with our names plastered directly next to our photographs, free for the taking.

But it is more than just names—consider the fae and their contracts and consent in the context of what are about to become the most terrifying words ever witnessed: "I agree to the terms and conditions." Consider those words in the context of a space where one cannot tell whether they are interacting with a living, sentient creature that wishes them ill, or at the very least is not invested or even particularly interested in their well-being. At least with massive corporations one can expect to blend in with the crowd; a faerie's attention is personal, which can bode either good or ill.

HOW TO UNSUBSCRIBE IF A FAERIE GETS YOUR EMAIL ADDRESS

Assuming that it is inconvenient to get an entirely new address and transfer over all your contacts, the safest option is to install a browser extension like FaeBlock or Saltline. However, if problems still occur, you may have to go to greater lengths—if your email server has the ability to set decorative background images, try using one with warding runes or sealing circles.

Should a faerie manage to outright hack your account, the most effective tactic is to ask several friends to spam your inbox with infinitely looping GIFs. We believe this works on the same principle as casting grains of wheat on the ground as a confusion and distraction tactic, so that the fae creature will have to stop to count them out individually, except of course a looping GIF will keep them permanently mesmerized.

Note: Be sure to talk to your parents and older loved ones about the dangers of answering emails from unknown contacts, especially those messages that claim you've received a holiday e-card from a distant relative.

HOW TO EXORCISE YOUR DEVICES

Draw an eight-pointed star—two interlocking squares—around the infested device. (It is fine to use newsprint or butcher paper for this; do not bother ruining your floors or tables with chalk.) Surround the star with a ring of salt, followed by a ring of rice. Set a lit candle inside each of the points of the star—this should only take a few minutes, so birthday candles are fine—and announce politely that you would like the faeries to leave. Extinguish the candles without touching them and leave the device in the circle until its battery runs out, at which point it may be safely retrieved. Be sure to keep pets and small children from disturbing the process.

Remember: An ounce of prevention is worth a pound of cure! If possible, keep a potted holly plant close by where you charge your device; otherwise, keeping the devices not currently in use on a surface made of holly or chestnut wood (or, in a pinch, cedar or maple) will serve. Himalayan rock salt lamps are an effective preventative measure as well, as long as they are kept in proximity (by which we mean no more than a foot away). These will also not be glaringly obvious and intrusive to guests.

Those We Brought with Us

The North American liminal ecology, at least in the modern world, has been hugely shaped by immigration, and then further shaped by the changing tides of modern life. From the wildly successful urban adaptation of the brownies, to the development or discovery of new creatures such as the Luck Pigeon, some faeries thrive in times of change, even as others are being slowly throttled to extinction.

BROWNIES

By far the most successful fae species to adapt to urban environments is the common brownie. Brownies are an invasive species native to the British Isles. Their physical size ranges from a handspan high to cat-sized. They have an almost human appearance, with the weathered skin of a farmer or a wind-chapped fisherman, though they are much hairier, with bulging features and weirdly delicate hands. Their eyes reflect light in the dark, and their teeth are sharp.

And, like many creatures of the liminal world, brownies exist not alongside humans, but because of and in balance with humans. The bargain they offer is one of the simplest: Leave out a little food for them, and they'll help in small ways. Traditional wisdom calls for a piece of bread and a saucer of milk, but in the modern world, mankind is so much more generous than that. Humans leave them *feasts*: bags and bags of scraps and leavings, garbage bins full of it, veritable landfills brimming with it.

In rural farming communities where the houses are spread out over miles, a home might have a single brownie in residence. In fact, in Britain of the 1600s and 1700s, superstitious families once considered it incredibly important to maintain a good relationship with their house brownie lest they wreak mischief: souring the milk, spoiling the butter, or causing the hens to stop laying. In urban environments, the difficulty comes not in maintaining a relationship with a brownie, but in forming one in the first place. Think of it in terms of stray cats—you can leave food out for them, but they aren't really yours until they know you as an individual. This would be difficult enough on its own, because the abundance of freely available food means the symbiotic relationship is no longer necessary for the brownies, but there is an additional complication—brownies, when they do form attachments to a territory, do so with the entire structure of a home or building. For someone living in a farmhouse, this doesn't matter, and would hardly even register as a problem. Someone living in an apartment building, however, as most city-dwelling people do, may have cause to question whether the investment of time, effort, and patience it would take to establish a relationship with a brownie is even worth it, as any benefits (e.g., lost buttons found, small tasks around the house completed, milk and bread lasting longer) are not guaranteed to be repaid to *them personally*. Their neighbors in the building stand an equal chance of receiving the benefits, without having to output any work.

Therefore, while brownies are a relatively harmless example of faerie species in urban environments, they are not generally worth the time spent finding and studying them.

THE TONTTU

Another species that has been unexpectedly affected by city living and apartment buildings is the tonttu, or sauna elf, which is native to Finland. Appearing as a tiny old man, the tonttu is not known to wreak mischief with particular malice. All he asks for is respect—sauna bathers should not throw too much water on the hot stones, nor let the sauna get dangerously warm, nor let the door swing open for too long so the heat gets out. Bathers also should finish their sauna early in the evening so the tonttu has privacy for himself. If the tonttu's generally reasonable requirements are not met, he may spend the night banging doors and kicking the walls in anger.

However, the tonttu, being traditionally minded, like most faeries, does not like the cramped quarters of the tiny electric saunas that are standard in Finnish apartments, so sightings have dropped significantly in recent decades.

REDCAPS

In the medieval era, redcaps were primarily found near the sites of battlefields, sometimes even years or decades afterward. While the common lore generally attests that they are drawn to any sort of widespread death (plagues, famine, etc.), scholars have confirmed that they are attracted to specifically violent deaths. There was no upsurge in redcap activity during the Spanish flu epidemic, for example, but even today there are areas of Europe where the casualties of the two World Wars drew enormous colonies of redcaps that have yet to begin dwindling in size. Further, there is evidence of former colonies of the North American variant of redcaps near mass graves in South and Central America. The physical land and humanity's collective social psyche still bear the scars of those years, and so, too, does the liminal world.

On a less massive scale, small colonies of redcaps have been documented at the sites of particularly gruesome murders or vehicular accidents. There is still some question within academic circles as to whether the redcaps are the cause of such events or the result; some scholars suggest that they may lie somewhere in between.

Redcaps range from the size of a squirrel to a large raccoon. They have a scuttling, scampering movement and are capable of running awkwardly on their back legs. They have a mangy, half-haired appearance, bulbous yellow eyes, unsettlingly human-like hands, and sharp teeth. The adult morph bears the characteristic red dorsal frill, which, if seen in dim light or unclearly, could easily be mistaken for a cap. They are obligate carnivores, but they will happily scavenge from carcasses if fresh prey isn't available. In rural environments, they subsist on small forest creatures, but in urban environments, they will hunt mammals as large as a medium-sized stray dog.

HULDUFÓLK

The huldufólk are grouped in a classification family with many of the common hill-type faeries of Western and Northern Europe, such as the common brownie. Huldufólk (Icelandic: "the hidden people") live inside rocks; they are gray colored and wear gray clothing, and like many other hill faeries, they are territorial and easily angered. Even today, Icelanders are cautious and respectful of the huldufólk when they are starting construction projects—if an expert believes a particular rock that is in the way of construction may be the home of the huldufólk, plans will have to be changed rather than destroy or disturb the rock, for fear of bringing the huldufólk's vengeance upon them. Traditional wisdom also forbids having sex beneath the Northern Lights, explaining that anyone who would be willing to do that with a person is probably one of the huldufólk in disguise, and that any child born from such a union would be a changeling.

Besides their native home, huldufólk are often commonly found in Minnesota, brought across the Atlantic by generations of Icelandic immigrants.

BLACK-DOGS

Once famously known as a harbinger of death and not uncommon for even non-scholars to observe in the wild (though only "superstitious" people generally recognize them for what they are), sightings of black-dogs have severely decreased since the 1950s, at least partially due to the noble work of animal welfare organizations in catching and neutering strays. However, a far more significant impact on this decrease occurred because of the huge advancements made in medical research in the last seventy years, particularly in regards to the development of effective vaccines in preventing millions of untimely deaths.

Despite this, some scholars do still note that there is a bump in recorded sightings of black-dogs during widespread epidemics (notably during the Spanish flu of 1918–1920, the 1974 smallpox outbreak in India, and the ongoing HIV/AIDS epidemic), though these numbers are potentially skewed due to confirmation bias: When an epidemic occurs, scholars tend to look harder for accompanying liminal creatures such as black-dogs.

Unlike the Luck Pigeon (see page 49), a black-dog does have an unsettling aura about it, easily noticed if the observer is paying attention. They are found throughout North America and the British Isles and come in many sizes and breed shapes, though most of them are large- to mid-sized mongrels. Any dog (of any color) can become a black-dog if it is left wild for long enough, though the exact causes and conditions are still unknown. Black-dogs are almost always found along roadways, and they tend to favor quieter, more deserted ones. If a black-dog smells incipient death upon a person, they will follow them for miles, or even days, walking when their target walks and stopping when they stop. There is also an element of self-fulfilling prophecy in play, as a person who notices that they are being followed by a black-dog (and recognizes it for what it is) will become increasingly distressed and even reckless, which sometimes leads to either a fatal accident or, regretfully, to suicide. However, it is worth remembering that the black-dog is not in itself a death sentence: There are several accounts of people noticing the black-dog, going to their doctors for a check-up, and discovering some condition that, if it had gone unnoticed, could have killed them in short order. There are also accounts of people who, fearing their death by manslaughter or murder, surrounded themselves with friends and protectors or otherwise took steps to remove themselves from the danger and escape their fate. In many cases, these people lived.

Whether the black-dog's target lives or dies, as soon as its business with the person has concluded in one way or another, the black-dog will peacefully depart, often so quietly that its absence goes unnoticed for some time. For its survivors, this is a welcome sign that the need for urgent vigilance has passed.

BLACK WITCH MOTH

Known by the same name and bearing a startling resemblance to the mundane species *Ascalapha odorata*, this liminal creature has long been known as a serious omen. In the Caribbean and Central America, it is believed to be a death omen at the very least, and always a general bearer of assorted calamities. On the other hand, in some parts of the Caribbean and the southern United States, being visited by a black witch moth is believed to be a sign of an upcoming monetary windfall. The best explanation scholars have been able to provide thus far is that the black witch moth is attracted somehow to an incipient change in fortunes, whether good or ill, just as mundane moths are attracted to lamps and other sources of light.

BANSHEES

Possibly the most famous death-related fae, banshees are always female and only visible to women (though, as detailed below, birth-assigned gender has no bearing on this). Banshees live "under-hill," referring to the burial mounds, cairns, and faerie hills that are found throughout the Irish countryside, the banshees' native habitat. While some banshee sightings have remarked upon the creature as being eerily tall, most of them describe the banshee as a stooped, ancient crone dressed in dark, filthy rags. Banshees are most famous for wailing and screaming outside the home of someone who is on death's door—a sure sign that there is no chance of recovery for someone suffering an illness or severe injury. Sometimes, if the dying person is particularly famous or powerful, the encroaching death is attended by several banshees.

Documented sightings of the banshee soared during the mid-1800s, when negligence, mismanagement, and criminal ignorance amongst the occupying British landholders resulted in the Great Hunger. (This event was otherwise known as the Irish Potato Famine, which was caused by a rotting plague that affected the single cultivar of potato grown in the country, wiping out years of crops from 1845 to 1852 and resulting in the deaths by starvation of more than one million citizens.)

CHANGELINGS
AND STOLEN CHILDREN

Traditional folklore tells us that from time to time, the faeries will take a shine to a particular infant or toddler, especially if the child is particularly beautiful or their parents are particularly boastful. In its place, the faeries are said to leave a changeling, which at first appears identical to the human child but eventually reveals its true nature. The simple fact of the matter is that the faeries do not leave changelings, period. Many modern scholars and psychologists believe that these myths and accounts were, in actuality, the only available explanation at the time for what we now suspect may have been the onset of autism symptoms—nearly all the identifying traits of "changelings" in myths map quite closely to many of the common presentations of the disorder in young children (including social disinterest, an aversion to touch and eye contact, a delay in speech acquisition or low rates of verbalization overall, highly focused and specific interests, lack of empathy, repetitive movements—even children on the less severe end of the spectrum, presenting only with a "dreamy" demeanor or not-quite-right social cues, have been described as "touched by the faeries"). Even in modern times, many parents of autistic children express a wish of wanting their "real child" back.

This is, obviously, a hugely damaging attitude to have, one that centers the feelings of the parents over the basic welfare of the child—but the "changeling" explanation in a historical context must have been better than the alternative of having no answers at all.

That said, creatures of the liminal world have been known to outright steal children without leaving a changeling to take their place—there are documented instances of this on every continent, some as simple as quiet little folktales whispered from family to family, some held up as explanations for a historical figure's great talents. Of the latter, one of the most plausible examples is the great warrior and renowned beauty Minamoto no Yoshitsune, who in his childhood (the mid-1100s, the end of Japan's Heian period) was hidden away in a Buddhist monastery to protect him from assassins and was thence kidnapped by a colony of tengu, the fierce and warlike bird-people of the remote mountain regions, who taught him martial arts and music before returning him to the human world. It was due to these supernatural gifts that Yoshitsune was able to defeat in single combat the supposedly greatest warrior in the land, Benkei, and gain his allegiance and fealty.

In this area, scholars encounter another obstacle due to the scanty amount of historical data available on missing persons—the data that we do have skews toward somewhat more affluent families in more populated areas, as they are 1) more likely to have resources to whom they can report a missing child, and 2) more likely to have those resources respond with sympathy and seriousness. Less privileged families and those in more rural areas are simply less likely to have their tragedies documented for posterity. For these reasons, we are once more uncertain whether the rate of faerie abduction has increased, decreased, or stayed the same over the past two or three hundred years.

LIBRARY FAERIES

There are at least 307 different documented pests in this category, some of which have been noted as far back as the 900s, most famously in the marginalia of the Canterbury 208 manuscript: "fucking bokewyrms getynge into the parchemin ageyn." Library faeries are as pervasive as earwigs and silverfish, and serious infestations can be far more damaging. While many varieties, such as the common paperwing, or the bokewyrm so infamously cursed by the unknown Canterbury monk, damage the physical aspect of the book (by chewing the edges for food, or by tearing off scraps with which to line a nest, or by burrowing through it), there are several varieties that damage books on the metaphysical level by destroying or damaging the information contained within. The inksucker faerie is the most well-known of this variety. It leaves pages intact—even the shape of the printed or written letters on the page is unchanged—but the reader's ability to *comprehend* the afflicted word is made difficult or impossible.

The best recommendation scholars currently have to prevent damage is to advise that public libraries maintain digitized backups of as much of their collections as possible. In the case of personal libraries or rare books where the object itself is as valuable as the information it contains, try storing books on shelves made of cedarwood or maple (rather than oak, pine, or birch). Whenever possible, these should be built with screws and hardware of raw iron, rather than chrome- or zinc-plated ones, as iron is well known to have naturally fae-repellent properties. There are some who claim that a well-made dovetail joint is also repellent to the fae, but there is no evidence to support this. In general, it is recommended that a collector identify which books may be particularly attractive to liminal creatures and isolate them from the rest of the collection, which will at least keep other books from becoming endangered by an infestation. Another historical method of protecting books (which, alas, would not be useful today) is to bind the book using leather made from the skin of a lamb that was thirty days old and killed on a full moon. (This was a popular method amongst medieval and ancient scholars of the fae for protecting their compiled books of notes, as it shields the text both from destructive liminal creatures and from human spies.)

If a book has already been metaphysically damaged, there are several potential methods of recovery. The easiest method is, of course, to simply cross-reference the page in question with another copy of the same text (hence the importance of digitizing collections, for many rare books are entirely unique). If a word has been rendered illegible but intact (as with the inksucker faerie's method), try isolating individual syllables or letters and writing them on a separate sheet of paper until the word is clear. A very badly damaged word may have to be rendered as individual *parts* of letters to make its meaning clear again, and the process may take several days, particularly if it is a very important word that carries a great deal of meaning in its sentence. In either case, when the missing word has been recovered, handwriting it onto the page with a silver-nib pen and iron gall ink will prevent the word from being taken again.

RECIPE FOR IRON GALL INK

Weigh a double handful of oak galls. Crush them into shards, and leave them to soak for several days in two or three cups of water, plus two tablespoons of red wine or vinegar. Strain out the shards and discard them. Into the remaining liquid, mix in one-fifth of the oak galls' weight of vitriol (aka copperas, aka ferrous sulfate). The brown liquid will instantly turn dark; add gum arabic in the same amount as the vitriol. Store in a tightly closed jar. Upon use, the translucent grayish ink will turn a rich black. This may be used for any material that must be protected from faerie damage, as the ferrous sulfate (iron salt) is repellent to them.

THE LUCK PIGEON

The Luck Pigeon is one of the poorest-documented liminal beings, but simultaneously it is also one of the most fascinating, perhaps because of its elusiveness, but most definitely because it is a supernatural creature that is limited exclusively to the urban environment of the last two hundred years.

It is a pigeon.

It looks like a pigeon. It coos like a pigeon. It walks like a pigeon, and it is weirdly unbothered by proximity to humans and will lazily leave off flying until the last possible moment, as pigeons do. It does not have a burning glint of malice in its eye that might give it away, nor a sparkle of faerie-dust along its wings, nor does it have a suspiciously concentrated pigeonly essence to set it apart from its kin.

It really is a pigeon. There is no way to know which pigeon in a flock it is, if any, and there seems to be only one at a time. Scholars hypothesize that immediately upon the death of The Pigeon, whatever force that makes it The Pigeon instantly transports to some other pigeon at a random location around the globe, whereupon that pigeon becomes The Pigeon. According to several social media groups exclusively devoted to locating The Pigeon (the Facebook group

"The The-Pigeon Fanciers," the Tumblr blog "thatbirbtho," the online forum PigeonWatch, and the Twitter hashtag #isthatthepigeon), as of this book's publishing, it may currently reside in or near Baltimore, Maryland.

The Pigeon would be a subject of great academic disagreement as to whether it genuinely counts as a supernatural entity of some sort, except for the fact that it so closely adheres to the pattern of interaction between fae and humans: If you mistreat or harass The Pigeon, you will suffer a rash of minor bad luck—spoiled milk, soured wine, missing a bus or subway by mere seconds, catching every red light when you're driving, etc. As a corollary, one should be able to conclude that gaining The Pigeon's favor through small gifts or pleasant manners would result in good luck, but as it is *a pigeon*, this is extraordinarily difficult to prove.

The Pigeon (or what we suspect to be The Pigeon) was temporarily captured by an amateur fae-spotter named Jennifer Mace in 2014. Mace's blog post ("you'll never guess what this fucking pigeon did to me," hosted on tumblr.com) went viral in the The Pigeon–tracking community and received hundreds of responses both attempting to debunk her claims or suggesting methods of conclusively proving whether the pigeon she had caged was indeed The Pigeon. Unfortunately, before any experts could contact her, Mace had released her captive pigeon into the wild once more. (She did not report an uptick of good or bad luck in the aftermath; if this was in fact The Pigeon, then presumably any ill favor she had gained by capturing it was canceled out by caring for it and releasing it.)

THE GREEN FAERIE: SPIRITS OF INEBRIATION

Intoxicants have long been used as a tool to access the world-beside-the-world. Whether by oracles breathing noxious vapors to attune themselves to prophecies and visions, or travelers drunkenly wandering off the road and into a faerie mound, when we find our inhibitions lowered, previously unseen doors creak open an inch or two. Faeries are born from the instinctive, unthinking parts of our consciousness—greed, lust, fury, or a bone-deep conviction of what is and is not fair. Intoxicants put us in closer contact with those parts of ourselves, and they push us a little ways out of the world.

Some of the most common faeries of inebriation include:

- ✳ **Whiskey:** shaped like shiny brown shoelaces, which wriggle at the edges of your vision
- ✳ **Gin:** silver-green bubbles, which float close to the floor
- ✳ **Tequila:** pure-white polygons, which make a noise like bees
- ✳ **Vodka:** misty, ghostlike, almost motionless blurs
- ✳ **Wine:** hallucinatory cups and mugs that always appear to be about to roll off the edge of a table

* **Beer:** brisk, bouncing marbles
* **Absinthe:** zingy green lights like fireflies; this is the origin of the name "the green fairy"
* **Marijuana:** slow-shimmering patches, which look like heat mirages
* **Cocaine:** thousands of microscopic specks, which glisten along the edges of objects, as if dipped in glitter
* **Opium (and its derivatives, including heroin, morphine, and laudanum):** slow-moving, iridescent purple-black clouds like an oil slick in midair

GHoST ToWNS

America has had a long history of strange, unexplained disappearances of people and places, sometimes even of entire towns. The first documented "ghost town" (a controversial term in the field, as ghosts do not exist) was the Roanoke Colony, whose inhabitants vanished without a trace at some point between 1588 and 1590.

Ghost towns in North America occurred most frequently in the Southwest, where a local gold rush could cause a boom in population and then just as quickly bust as soon as the gold vein was tapped out. Many of the miners working in these boom towns were Chinese immigrants and, as has been previously mentioned, humans moving in great numbers tend to inadvertently bring things along with them. This led to one of the most terrifying accounts of the 1880s, the zombie infestation of Promise Ridge, Nevada.

The zombies in question were, we know now, the Chinese jiāngshī (殭屍, or in Cantonese: goengl-sil), often translated as "hopping zombie" and most famously documented by the scholar Ji Xiaolan (1724–1805). Jiāngshī are a "spirit" (by which we mean a liminal being that is intangible and usually invisible) that has been possessed and reanimated a corpse. Oftentimes, these corpses are stiff with rigor mortis, or already partially decayed, and so the spirit moves about with a lurching, hopping motion that is, by all accounts, dreadful to behold. Jiāngshī hide in small, dark locations during the day and emerge at night; they kill people and animals to absorb their qi (life energy). A person who has been injured by a jiāngshī will decline slowly over the course of several days while their qi is gradually sapped away until, at last, they die. A person who dies this way will often become a new jiāngshī themselves.

Just as other liminal species were carried from one place to another, jiāngshī were brought to Promise Ridge by its large population of Chinese immigrants, who began settling the area in the mid-1800s. The jiāngshī were documented in great detail in the town's local English-language newspaper, the *Ridge Reporter*, which printed its first story on the infestation, "Outlying Farms Struck by Illness," on May 18, 1883: "We are grieved to announce that several family members of the Yost and Hawke farms have passed away, having suffered from a wasting illness that struck suddenly several weeks ago. . . ." This was followed over the next eight months by three other similar stories from the *Reporter*. By November, the *Reporter* had named the alleged illness "the Promise Plague," and seventy-two people were reported to have died from it (all of them white, as the *Reporter* only printed obituaries for its white residents).

However, extensive investigation of microfiche copies of Promise Ridge's Chinese-language newspaper, *Promise Ridge Weekly*, reveal that it had alerted its readers to the presence of a possible jiāngshī in March, two months before it came to the *Reporter*'s attention. The following issue of the *Weekly* included a short essay from the monk of the town's Taoist temple about the best ways to protect oneself from the creature. (Talisman papers, rice chaff, a variety of different amulets and sigils, the smell of vinegar, strategically placed mirrors, crowing roosters, ringing bells, and red mung beans are only a few of the protective measures mentioned in the monk's essay.)

The so-called Promise Plague continued for the next four years, and more than five hundred deaths were attributed to it in the obituaries of the *Ridge Reporter*. However, in August of 1887 the plague of jiāngshī suddenly boomed into a full infestation, and more than two thousand people were killed over the course of a week. By the following week, the survivors had fled, carrying to the towns hundreds of miles around terrifying stories of hauntings and dreadful leaping creatures attacking out of nowhere. Promise Ridge became, abruptly, a ghost town. People attempting to return and investigate the abandoned gold mines were never heard from again.

Travel and the Open Road

An essential part of the nebulous, abstract idea of "Americana" is the symbol of the open road and what it represents. There are a few scholars who have attempted to prove that there is some kind of nigh-supernatural impulse seeped into the land itself, the compulsion to move simply for the sake of moving—*l'appel du voie*, perhaps, if readers will excuse my poor French grammar.

In any case, the open road is one of the closest places where we can access the liminal world—it, too, is a place-between-places where strange things can happen and the rules are not quite the same as in normal life.

Vehicle Superstitions and Road Trips

Ley lines are often influenced by popular travel routes, which means that the map of North America's ley lines is a fairly close match to that of its freeways—or perhaps it is the other way around, with the freeways following ley lines. In either case, the open expanse of continent compels movement and travel—nowhere else in the world has quite the culture of road trips that North America has.

Simple air spirits (collectively known as zephyrs, from the Greek god Zephyrus, god of the west wind) find freeways particularly enticing, due to the buffeting gusts of passing vehicles. These zephyrs, like ether sprites, are all but invisible, and tend to move about in flocks of a few dozen. When glimpsed from the corner of your eye, they appear like birds made of long, trailing ribbons.

However, there are many more dangerous species that prey upon zephyrs as part of the natural food chain, and these can be rather more troublesome to humans. Some people have reported feeling an eerie sense of unease that compels them to check their car's rearview mirror again and again, certain that there must be someone in the back seat.

Motorcyclists have even more harrowing stories of suddenly sensing a presence riding along on the seat behind them. These road-spirits (scholars do not yet have a categorical classification for them) have been known to cause accidents, but motorcyclists are a practical bunch and have independently developed certain useful wards against this creature's devious and malicious tricks. The most effective seems to be hanging a silver bell somewhere on the vehicle, as the chiming drives the creature away in torment.

The Wild Hunt:
Then and Now

In the pre-industrial era, people in rural eras of the British Isles would occasionally report hearing a hunting party passing through in the night, usually along disused paths in the forest, though occasionally venturing through a village as it slumbered. Those who were reckless enough to peek through their shutters or creep into the forest told tales of fine Seelie lords and ladies laughing and singing, wearing beautiful (if slightly old-fashioned) clothing that glimmered like starlight, seated on white horses that were saddled and bridled and shod with silver. The Wild Hunt ventured out from time to time on the new or full moon, either in the height of summer or the depth of winter (July and January, respectively, for the less poetic-minded reader).

After the advent of the railroad, nearly all sightings of the Wild Hunts ceased, probably due to the interference between the iron rails and ley lines. However, in recent years, scholars have begun noticing certain parallels between the Wild Hunts of yore and a much more modern phenomenon.

Twenty or thirty years after the worldwide proliferation of rail travel, people began witnessing what they called "ghost trains." These trains traveled exclusively by night, usually during the new or full moon, most often in the height of summer and the depth of winter.

How interesting! scholars of liminal phenomena reasoned. Something brand-new. This assumption, and the scientific conclusions that were based on it, persisted until three factors turned this theory on its head:

1. The invention of high-speed photography
2. A great number of CCTV cameras that overlook railroad tracks
3. Rail travel being gradually abandoned across America while many of the railroads fall into disrepair and, critically, rust

Faeries cannot touch cold iron or steel. This is an undisputable fact, one of the first that scholars of the fae learn when beginning their studies. However, once the metal begins to rust, its power dwindles, and there are several fae creatures who are then able to encourage the process at a quicker rate. Mainland Europe and Britain have maintained an active rail system since the Industrial Revolution, and subsequently, the friction of the trains' wheels on the tracks keeps the rust off—and the fae away. But in America, the rail system, for the most part, has fallen into disrepair.

And once the rust settles in, the railroad becomes, essentially, another form of a ley line, a conduit for power to flow along. Thence: ghost trains, running along the rusted, overgrown tracks that wind, forgotten, through forests and along cornfields.

Rekka Theodore, a fae-spotter who specializes in high-speed photography, managed to capture pictures of the interior of one of these ghost trains for the first time on the night of January 22, 2010. By 2016, she had developed a network of cameras that allowed her to digitally reconstruct a three-dimensional imaging of an entire car of one of these trains. To the general surprise of academia, her photographs and images showed what appeared to be a cocktail party: elegant, beautiful ladies and gentlemen wearing fine (if somewhat old-fashioned, vaguely 1920s-styled) clothing that glittered like starlight, sitting inside a train car that appeared to be made of solid silver, drinking wine that in the photographs seems to gleam with its own light.

THE GENTLEMAN AT THE CROSSROADS

Like in many other areas of academic research, scholars of the fae are primarily limited by historical documentation: It is not known how many crossroads in the pre-industrial world were considered significant, nor how many of them fostered crossroads-demons. Scholars do not even know what else to call them: "demon" is, of course, a misnomer too closely tied to religious mythology to be accurate—another downfall of our documentation. Throughout history, people gave them a name that made sense to them within their context and limited understanding. With more information now available to us, we shall call them, then, the Gentlemen at the Crossroads.

Documentation before the modern era comes through stories and hearsay, but the one benefit that scholars of lore have over other areas of academia is that myth *is* our business. In her seminal 1983 essay "An Abundance of Crossroads, a Dearth of Bargains," Edith Martlet assembles an image of the Gentleman at the Crossroads with descriptions drawn from a cross-section of mythology: a slender man, often dark of hair and eyes, he is cordial, courteous, gracious, immaculately dressed, and always well spoken. The folkloric canon consistently mandates that the Gentleman waits by the crossroads at midnight, in the dark of the moon or the full. In fact, moon phase has nothing to do with it, but the crossroads themselves *are* important.

There was definitely a Gentleman on Ellis Island from at least 1902 to 1914, the peak years of its operation, during which time thousands of people per day were processed through its halls. Scholars are fairly certain that his presence lasted well into the mid-1950s, though documented sightings fell sharply after the end of World War I. A Gentleman's territory doesn't necessarily need to be a literal intersection of two streets, though evidence suggests that it does have to be related to travel in some way. Moreover, the busier and more influential a crossroads, the more power its Gentleman can draw upon, as some creatures draw upon ley lines or other sources. And we know that in the people the Gentlemen approach, there is always an element of desperation. That, too, is in the historical documentation, for who else in the pre-industrial era would go to a crossroads at midnight except those who had been driven to the very limits of their ability to endure?

Upon meeting his client (for one cannot technically call them victims), the Gentleman greets them politely, makes idle conversation, determines what is troubling them most, and asks: *What are you willing to do to make all this go away? What are you willing to give up in exchange for your heart's desire?* A struggling musician might ask for fame and fortune; a young lady wronged by love might ask for revenge.

There is one figurative form of crossroads where we might expect to find a Gentleman and consistently fail to do so: airports. Airports should fit all the requirements, should they not? A place between places; a stop on a journey to somewhere else; thousands of people passing through every day; a sense of dread and desperation. Where are the Gentlemen asking weary and worried travelers, *Something terrible is happening, are you going to make it home in time? What would you give for that?* But for whatever reason, we don't find them there. Too much light at all hours of the day, perhaps? Too few corners for a private conversation? Too much iron and technology?

On the road, Gentlemen can be found at truck stops, in rural gas stations, and in state welcome centers. Their once-immaculate clothes are now faded and ill-fitting. In cities, they are found on street corners, bundled in old sweaters and threadbare winter jackets, dull-eyed and hungry and crammed in too close together to thrive. But still they ask, *Who are you? What is it that you want? What will you give to get it?*

Be careful what you wish for. Be careful how you answer.

FAMOUS LOCAL CRYPTIDS OF THE WORLD

Cryptids, the common name for liminal creatures that do not show human-like intelligence, are one of the most frequently sighted supernatural beings amongst laymen. Ordinary people (not scholars of the liminal world, in other words) are usually *slightly* more willing to entertain the idea of a cryptid's existence—especially a local cryptid—than they are of higher-order beings. Cryptids generally do not possess great supernatural powers, and their appearance, although sometimes remarkable, does not fall outside the bounds of what would be realistic or possible for a mundane creature. The Loch Ness Monster is a prime example of this category—many people who would firmly consider themselves too "rational" to accept the existence of faeries are quite happy to profess a belief in Nessie, and some have even reported sightings of it themselves.

Following is a list of sixteen of the most famous local cryptids of the world, excluding the very, very famous (the yeti, the aforementioned Loch Ness Monster, and the Sasquatch, for example).

1. **Sewer alligators (New York City, USA):** "Alligators" seems to be a term of convenience rather than accuracy. Large reptiles, very elusive, often albino.

2. **The Nameless Thing of Berkeley Square (London, UK):** Strong malevolent energy (possibly demonic?), responsible for several deaths.

3. **Grandfather Boroda (Moscow, Russia):** Elderly bearded man in a fur coat and hat, possibly a spirit of ice or winter. His touch leaves instant frostbite.

4. **Mamlambo, the Brain Sucker (Johannesburg, South Africa):** Possibly related to the sewer alligators of New York City. A large river-dwelling reptile, known for gnawing the heads of its victims.

5. **Bhootbilli, the Ghost Cat (Pune, India):** A medium-sized creature that appears to be some sort of mammal, larger than a dog but smaller than a lion, possibly cat-shaped. Known for preying upon small animals and pets.

6. **Raiju (Iwate Prefecture, Japan):** A spirit of thunder and lightning, often described as wolf- or weasel-shaped, though it often appears as a ball of crackling electricity (possibly related to St. Elmo's fire?).

7. **Ucumar (Argentina):** This elusive creature seems to dwell mostly in the remote mountains, though it is sometimes sighted in settled areas, where it is known to prey on children

and pets. Almost certainly related to the Sasquatch of North America, the Yiren of China, the yeti of the Himalayas, and the yowie of Australia.

8. **The Dark Something (Los Angeles, USA):** This being emits insidious malevolent energy. It was bound in iron chains and trapped beneath the Angels Flight funicular railway in 1937 by a small team of amateur "occultists," led by Dr. Elizabeth Derochea, who had previously made several appeals to the city zoning board and animal control about the creature.

9. **Maltese Tiger (Fujian Province, China):** Extremely elusive, very little modern documentation. Reported as being markedly larger than mundane tigers, with blue-gray fur and dark stripes.

10. **The Lady in the Boat (Nice, France):** A lady in a white dress, spotted frequently since the 1850s. Responsible for several deaths—always young men under the age of forty, always by drowning.

11. **The Golden Swordfish (Venice, Italy):** An exceptionally large fish, vaguely resembling a swordfish and appearing to be made of solid gold with jewels for eyes. Said to be an omen of great fortune, particularly in mercantile ventures.

12. **The Great Jackal (Cairo, Egypt):** Possibly related to the Grims or black-dogs of the British Isles, whose appearance heralds death; if so, almost certainly linked to ancient worship of the god Set.

13. Restless spirits (Chefchaouen, Morocco): The prison of Chefchaouen's citadel, located at the conjunction of two major local ley lines, houses several trapped spirits. It is unknown whether they are the ghosts of past prisoners or whether they are liminal creatures (possibly very weak djinn). Locals avoid this place.

14. Taniwha (New Zealand): Sometimes seen as a guardian, sometimes as a predator, these spiny-backed creatures live in the water, especially near areas with strong currents or submerged rocks that could be deadly to swimmers and boaters.

15. Naga fireballs (Phon Phisai, Thailand): Annually on Wan Ok Phansa (the last night of Vassa, occasionally known as Buddhist Lent), the naga (river-serpent spirits) of the Mekong River release small fireballs, previously known as "ghost lights," which rise from deep below the surface of the water to float hundreds of feet above it. A very popular tourist occasion.

16. Lau (South Sudan): A giant aquatic serpent, reportedly up to one hundred feet long with a distinctive loud, booming call that has been compared to a trumpeting elephant. It is known to aggressively attack boats, as well as people and livestock who stray too close to the banks of the rivers in which it dwells. It is probably related to the lukwata of Lake Victoria in Uganda.

Native Species of North America

In addition to the large number of creatures that have been brought to this continent by centuries of colonists and immigrants, there has of course always been a rich and vibrant ecology of native species. Many have been driven from their natural habitats by urban sprawl, and many more are in danger of extinction due to the environmental impact of more aggressive transplant species, so conservation is an ongoing issue amongst scholars. It is worth noting, too, that past generations of scholars have not done as much to promote conservation and care as they should have, since they viewed America's native liminal ecology as expendable, to one degree or another. These attitudes have still not been completely driven out of academia, but the burgeoning popularity of fae-spotting amongst amateurs and hobbyists is, at least, bringing to light a great deal of awareness of these crucial issues.

It is a great tragedy that the supernatural ecology of North America has been so cataclysmically overrun with invasive species. It serves as a mirror of the other great cataclysm of the continent over the last half millennium: the European colonists' genocide against Native American peoples.

Despite how thoroughly this bloody history and its victims have been erased from modern society's consciousness, Native American liminal beings still exist and this encyclopedia would be the poorer for perpetuating that erasure. The following entries by no means constitute a full list—it does not even scratch the surface. There are thousands of species of liminal beings on the North American continent still in existence today, though many are critically endangered. There are likely hundreds of thousands more that have already been lost, either to extinction or because they have been forgotten as a result of hundreds of years of devaluation and outright suppression of Native knowledge. Amongst mainstream academia, the study of the liminal world has been discredited since the Enlightenment, often mocked as mere childish folly—it is only now, with advancements in technology providing more conclusive ways of documenting proof, that the field is beginning to make any kind of progress in repairing its reputation and establishing itself as a legitimate and important field of study. And yet, despite the intensely personal experience of having their knowledge and life's work discounted, scholars in this field have for centuries still held *exactly* the same attitude toward Native experts, decrying their factual observations as mere "superstition," rejecting their contributions in order to lift up their own work and their own egos, and seeing nothing repugnant or hypocritical in their own behavior and prejudices. In fact, Native experts hold an intimate, practical knowledge of these creatures, partially because they have generally accepted these beings as a known and real part of their environment—just as rural folk of the British Isles once knew brownies to be quite real, and felt it imperative to treat them with honor and generosity.

In recent years, faerie scholarship has at last begun to acknowledge the vast amount of potential contributions that Native peoples and other marginalized groups can make to the field. However, the key word there is "begun"—this field, like many others of academia, is still dominated by white, upper- and middle-class men. But perhaps there is some hope that this field can change for the better more quickly than other branches of academia. While every area of scholarship can benefit from a rich variety of minds and backgrounds bringing new perspectives to the conversation, the study of liminal beings practically demands it. There are fae creatures of the world that have literally never been documented by a white male scholar, despite decades and centuries of study.

Indeed, there are some species that are impossible for certain demographics to see even when they're in the same room as them. For instance, consider the findings of the biologist Jean Blakeman, who in 1942 conclusively proved, first, that she had captured a banshee, and, second, that her male colleagues found it impossible to gaze directly at the creature, notice it, or, even after having it pointed out directly, remember specifics of what it looked like. (Famously, the one "exception" to this pattern was L. M. Yarrow, Blakeman's young undergraduate assistant, who came out as a trans woman fifty years later.)

If we already have examples of liminal beings concealing themselves from entire demographics of people, should we not endeavor to have as many different kinds of eyes on our data as possible? And, moreover, should we not strive to create spaces for the people who have been saying for centuries already, "We've been trying to tell you, when will you listen?"

THE AKEKI
(OR WESTERN BROWN PIXIE)

The "western brown pixie" (common English name; Latin: *Nympharum akeki*), a native species of the western coast of the United States, is not actually a pixie. European settlers and early naturalists of the mid-1800s mistakenly classified the western brown pixie based on observations of the Old World species that they were more familiar with, and while there are similarities and parallels in terms of behavior and preferred environment between the two creatures, the anatomical differences should be obvious even to a hobbyist observer—notably the size, wing shape, and proportion of limbs. The species is more accurately known as akeki, or pain-spirit, according to the lore of the Native American tribes of the Western United States, including the Achumawai and Atsugewi.

Like the European pixies they were previously compared to, akeki nest in small colonies or hives like bees and wasps. Their nests, which are generally made of mud and tree bark or leaves, have historically been extremely well camouflaged and difficult to locate, as they are only the size of a basketball, and usually located high in the crowns of trees. However, due to the effects of climate change bringing warmer and drier winters, there have been reports of more than thirty "superhives" scattered across Northern California, quite similar to the giant wasp nests that have become increasingly common in the southeastern region of the country. While akeki rarely actually *infest* suburban homes, they have been known to scavenge chips of wood from clapboard-sided houses (damage that is usually ascribed to termites) and they do sometimes build nests in abandoned wooden structures in more rural locations.

As with both wasps and pixies, akeki should be approached with caution, as in large groups they can be dangerous or even deadly. Both lore and modern observation warn that the akeki can cause sharp physical pain and illness, including disorientation, amnesia, and other symptoms of "madness." We suggest avoiding the pursuit of this species unless accompanied or advised by an experienced Native medicine person.

PUKWUDGIE

Native to the northeastern coastal states and particularly the traditional homeland of the Wampanoag, this species is generally classified in the same scientific family as the European brownie, West African aziza, and other cousin species. Pukwudgies appear almost human-like, though they are smaller and very hairy. Like their counterparts elsewhere in the world, they are known to be quite elusive—it has long been suspected they have the ability to turn invisible, though modern scholars have suggested that these forest dwellers are in fact using supremely excellent camouflaging. Again like their cousin species, while pukwudgies are sometimes known to be helpful and beneficial to humans, they have a low tolerance for interference and are easily annoyed. However, the pukwudgie is unique in that it adds fire-starting to the list of magical mischief that it will visit upon someone who has haplessly offended it.

The pukwudgie is a severely endangered species, due to the growth in human population density in its natural habitat. It has a strong preference for wild woodlands, and the steady destruction of these environments as human settlements encroach on what was once remote has caused a worrying drop in sightings of them in recent decades.

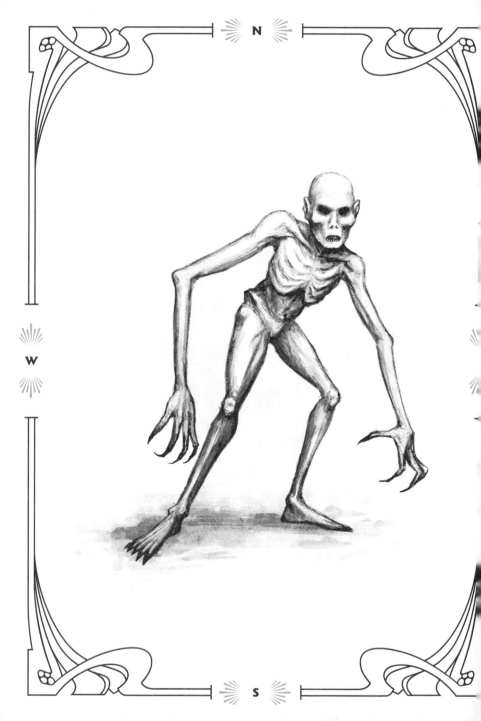

WENDIGO

Of the liminal species native to North America, the wendigo is one of the most dangerous predators. Amongst the Algonquin peoples, who are spread across Eastern and Central Canada and the Great Lakes, wendigo are universally known to be monstrous and malevolent. The wendigo is a creature of profound hunger, so much so that it has become a symbol not only of horrific appetites, but also the sort of unsatisfiable greed, obsession, and selfishness that unquestionably crosses the border into outright antisocial, community-destroying behaviors.

Wendigo are large but gaunt, even skeletal. Their skin is gray and ashy, and their bones protrude from filthy skin stretched drum-tight over atrophied muscles. Wendigo are vaguely human-shaped, having two arms, two legs, and the ability to walk upright. Their limbs are unnaturally long, giving them terrifying speed, and they have the ability to move silently through even difficult underbrush. They often appear in times of famine, and they are known to hunt humans without provocation and eat them, sometimes tracking and toying with their unlucky victims for days before attacking—this suggests that wendigo, like boggarts, may be partially timorvorous (feeding on fear), though they are definitively and primarily ravenous for raw human flesh.

There are accounts, too, of humans turning into wendigo when the pangs of starvation drove them to cannibalism, but as there have been no attestations of this in the entire twentieth century, scholars are hesitant to draw conclusions either for or against this hypothesis—more data is required, but understandably, no one is particularly eager to go searching for it.

PSONEN

Found seasonally in the northeast region of the continent, this species is one that scholars of the fae, in partnership with Abenaki medicine keepers, have been watching particularly closely for the past decade, due to the suspected impact of climate change on the psonen's behaviors and habitats.

Psonen are eagle-sized birds that can, with a beat of their wings, cause snowstorms and icy winds, both as a method of self-defense against predators and as a side effect of increased flight during their mating season (late December through February). While for several years it was feared that climate change would cause severe damage to the psonen's population numbers, scholars are recently noticing an interesting trend—the frequency of severe winter weather events, such as polar vortices in the Northeast, has coincided with a *rise* in the population numbers, not a decrease. Psonen were once documented to mate roughly once every five to seven years, but it is now suspected that higher summer temperatures are causing the psonen to reproduce more frequently—even as regularly as annually, though this data has yet to be conclusively confirmed. Though this may at first seem like a good thing, it raises a new concern: overcrowding of the psonen's habitats. As with any imbalance of population numbers, this will certainly cause cascading effects through the rest of the food chain, but the more immediate worry is that of their effect on the weather. Larger and larger mating flights of hundreds or even thousands of psonen could bring about a truly cataclysmic winter storm. Unfortunately, due to the public's general apathy toward issues of climate change and the general misconception that creatures like the psonen do not exist, there is neither enough funding nor personnel to launch any kind of system that would endeavor to bring the population back under control.

THUNDERB**I**RD

"Thunderbird" is the collective name for a group of related species that span a significant majority of the North American continent. Thunderbirds are also distantly related to the psonen (and possibly very, *very* distantly related to the giant roc of the Middle East, which was hunted to extinction in the sixteenth century). Resembling giant eagles with black-and-white-patterned wings, thunderbirds are so large that the northwestern species has been known to pluck fully grown whales from the sea with their talons. This has not been witnessed since the 1930s, due to the catastrophic plunge in the population numbers of many major whale species as a result of the whaling industry. The thunderbirds' population, once numbering an estimated ten thousand individuals, also was decimated in response to this, and now barely tops a mere five hundred. Were they not so long-lived (roughly three hundred to four hundred years), thunderbird species across North America may well have ended up going extinct for lack of sufficient food. However, as whale populations have begun to stabilize and recover since the 1980s, scholars are hopeful that this will result in a recovery of the thunderbird population as well.

Because of their huge size, thunderbirds have only a few natural enemies. The main competitor of the Great Lakes thunderbird (aka the Algonquin thunderbird) is the mishipeshu (see page 97), while that of the Western thunderbird (aka the Sioux thunderbird) is a species of horned serpent known locally as Unhcegila—both are water dwellers. Like their wintry cousin the psonen, thunderbird species often have powers over the weather.

DEER WOMAN

Native to the eastern woodlands and the Midwest, this creature appears in the form of a beautiful human woman with the legs (or at least hooves) of a deer. Some tribes believe that the Deer Woman was once a human woman who gained supernatural powers after being sexually assaulted and murdered, and there is clearly documented evidence that the Deer Woman's behavior regarding humans is skewed significantly toward the benevolent when interacting with women and the malevolent when interacting with men.

In her kindlier state, the Deer Woman has been known to help women and girls who seek them out for assistance, whether with love, fertility, or revenge against men who have harmed them. Against these men, the Deer Woman becomes vicious and deadly—she lures murderers, rapists, abusers, cheaters, and other toxic men into the woods with her beauty, where she crushes them with her hooves or curses them to a slow wasting death of yearning. In this way, the Deer Woman serves a similar function to North American society as worship of the Furies did to the ancient Greeks.

GRANTS AND FELLOWSHIPS

The Deer Woman is one of the liminal creatures mentioned in the guidelines of the Amy Hahn Scholarship, which provides one of the most generous research grants to women scholars of the liminal world who are focusing their studies on the categories of creatures that would be inaccessible to their male counterparts. Other creatures mentioned include, but are not limited to, banshees, the Furies, harpies, nymphs, dryads, sirens, and selkies.

KUSHTAKA
(KÓOSHDAAKAA)

Categorized with other animal-humanoid shapeshifters, the kushtaka is a species native to southeast Alaska (home of the Tlingit nation). While there are a few stories of kushtaka being helpful toward humans, the general consensus is that they are dangerous, manipulative, fiercely intelligent, terrifyingly fast, and fond of playing tricks—often fatal ones—on the unwary. By imitating the screams and cries of women or infants, kushtaka lure their victims into rivers and bays to drown them, consume their souls, or turn them into a new kushtaka, a slow process from which victims have occasionally been rescued, though few ever fully recover. According to traditional knowledge and the documentation of generations of Tlingit scholars and shamans, the kushtaka have the ability to shapeshift into nearly any form, though they seem to have an affinity for taking the shape of river otters. The kushtaka's sadistic temper can potentially be appeased with gifts, especially tobacco, but this is unreliable and very risky. In general, it is better to keep a careful defense to ward off kushtaka. For this, dogs are the best option, first because they are able to sense or smell the presence of a kushtaka well before a human is able to, and second because the kushtaka have a profound fear of them.

Tlingit history tells us that the kushtaka caused a landslide just north of Thomas Bay in 1750, a disaster that killed more than five hundred people and led to the area being known amongst locals as the Bay of Death (*Geey Nana* in the Tlingit language). Due to the extensive expanses of wilderness in Alaska that provide space for colonies of kushtaka to continue to thrive, sightings of the creatures (and accidents because of them) have continued steadily into recent times. Because a kushtaka has never been successfully captured for study, and because of their fearsome and ever-changing appearance, scholars are as yet unsure how they are being affected by climate change or how the ecology of southeast Alaska might be affected if the kushtaka were to be eliminated from the local food chain.

MISHIPESHU

The mishipeshu is a lake-dwelling creature, resembling a great cat, but horned and covered with scales rather than fur. While it is definitively reptilian, due to this strong feline resemblance, the mishipeshu is sometimes known as the Great Lynx or water panther, though people unfamiliar with the lore have also mistaken it for a dragon. Like many beings of the liminal world, the mishipeshu has an unpredictable nature—if given offerings and treated with reverence, it can bestow favorable magical help, including protecting travelers on the Great Lakes from storms and driving shoals of fish into fishermen's nets. However, it is just as commonly known to cause those great storms—even in mundane circles, people have described hurricanes on the Lakes as "coming out of nowhere" and reported feeling a strange, almost malicious presence emanating from the water, though usually they ascribe that energy as coming from the water itself rather than to any creature within it.

The most famous disaster that is hypothesized to have been related to the activity of the mishipeshu is the wreck of the SS *Edmund Fitzgerald* on November 10, 1975. Scholars also suspect that the Mataafa Storm of November 27–28, 1905, a cyclone across the

Great Lakes that wrecked no fewer than twenty ships and damaged nine others, may have been caused by the creatures as well. (There are many scholars who are eager to ascribe every Great Lakes storm to the mishipeshu without further supporting evidence, seemingly ignorant of the fact that weather also sometimes happens by itself without supernatural involvement. Even the origins of these two disasters are merely theories.)

The American South

No review of the landscape of the American liminal ecology would be complete without discussing the South. For too long, academic study of the region's faeries has been wracked by either near-total erasure or by euphemism, so let it be said plainly: The faerie ecology of the American South has been overwhelmingly shaped by the transatlantic slave trade.

There is no value (either academic or, frankly, moral) in attempting to dodge this issue, though of course there are milksop scholars who attempt to talk around it when they are forced to discuss it at all, and prefer to summarize the region's faerie population merely as containing "high numbers of African transplant species" before moving along to areas that are less uncomfortable for them to subject to the scrutiny of disciplined research. Not only is this criminally lazy academia, it is a grave and ongoing insult to the entire region, its residents, and its history.

As with the historical violence that so strongly impacted the continent's population of native species of liminal creatures, this is a deeply fraught subject and we cannot do justice to it in a few pages of a single book. There are reams and reams of scholarly writing on the beings of Europe and Asia; there is the potential for reams of scholarly writing on those of Africa, the Caribbean, Brazil, and the American South, too. If these few scant pages are worth anything at all, they are merely a single drop (if that!) in the very, very large barrel of potential study.

ADZE

A spirit, usually appearing in the form of a small insect, native to the forests and coastal wetlands of Ghana and Togo. Because of its propensity to take such a tiny form, it has the ability to wriggle its way through any wards or defenses around a home. The adze bites its victims on any bare flesh they have left exposed as they sleep and sucks their blood. Victims of this creature, as with those attacked by other vampiric beings, often fall sick (generally showing malaria-like symptoms), and their health declines over the course of several days. Victims of heartier constitutions sometimes recover, though they often do not fully regain their former vitality; those who are at higher risk, such as young children, the already ill, and the elderly, are in danger of death if intervention is not taken immediately (with modern medicine, blood transfusions and supportive care are effective until the danger has passed). Adze are undeniably of liminal descent, but they have little natural intelligence or motives beyond instinctive hunger, and therefore cannot be bargained with. Adze also occasionally have been known to possess humans (similar to the Chinese jiāngshī, though the adze cannot reanimate corpses), but this seems to be quite rare and such an occurrence has not been reported in more than fifty years.

Adze prefer tropical temperatures—in North America, they're rarely found north of Georgia or west of Louisiana—though their range has been slowly growing due to climate change bringing warmer, milder winters to more northerly locations.

TOKOLOSHE

The tokoloshe is quite small, only about the size of a child, and has an unsettlingly primate-like appearance, with long bony fingers and mangy hair all over its body. Native to South Africa (and now found in some of the more temperate areas of the American South), it is one of the more immediately lethal liminal species, possessing the ability to kill a sleeping person without waking them or their loved ones, without leaving a mark, and without making a sound. Notably, the tokoloshe only kills those who sleep on the ground or a very low bed near a warm fire. Much like boggarts (mentioned earlier in this book), the tokoloshe actively delight in malevolence, sometimes forgoing outright murder in favor of terrifying their victims to death, waking them by sitting on their chests or strangling them.

However, tokoloshe are somewhat easier to manage than boggarts and others of their type—the easiest way to protect oneself from tokoloshe attacks in the night is simply to elevate one's bed to hip-height or higher, though even a brick or two under each leg of the bedframe is often enough to confound them. If an area is particularly troubled by an infestation of tokoloshe, a sangoma—a practitioner of traditional medicine amongst the Zulu people—may have to be called in to drive them out. On the other hand, tokoloshe are easily summoned by witches or people seeking vengeance, and can be made cooperative with the person's will by leaving them gifts of soured milk.

KONDERONG

Appearing as small, scrawny humans with very, very long beards that they wear wrapped around their bodies like clothing, the konderong are best known for having backward feet (a feature that has popped up frequently enough across the world's liminal ecologies that scholars are still arguing about whether to reorganize the entire classification system based on this [see also: the Filipino aswang, the ancient Roman antipode (extinct), etc.]). The konderong are originally native to the Senegalese bush, which experiences warm temperatures all year round—in the Americas, they are not found farther north than central Georgia, and they thrive much more successfully in Florida, Mexico, Brazil, and through the Caribbean. The species is incredibly elusive, and even experienced field scholars have a very difficult time spotting them without the use of special equipment or a touch of second sight.

As with other liminal creatures of their type, the konderong are capricious, short-tempered, and prone to causing small mischiefs, such as prompting someone carrying an unwieldy load to lose their balance and spill their burden, making objects much heavier or lighter than expected, chasing away wild game from hunters, or striking someone temporarily blind. Their most dangerous aspect by far, however, is their proclivity for stealing children.

Like other trickster types, though konderong cause annoyance and trouble, they also bring with them the potential for great reward: According to traditional lore, each konderong carries a calabash that can produce infinite wealth and material goods upon request. Modern scholars are uncertain about the mechanism of this, as no konderong has been successfully captured for study in modern times. Clues found in folklore, however, suggest that wealth produced by the calabash would follow the patterns of other species' magically produced faerie-gold: merely dry leaves disguised as money, which returns to its original state after several days apart from its creator.

STOLEN CHILDREN

In 1813, while visiting relatives in South Carolina, the anthropologist and naturalist Charlotte Baer recorded in her journal that the people enslaved by her hosts seemed to be "quite superstitious," to the point that one of the women had attempted to "give away her newborn infant to the fairies" the night previously. However, this account cannot and should not be considered as a reliable source—Baer was a white woman of well-to-do background with very little (if any) personal contact with the people she was observing, and likely no knowledge whatsoever of their history, culture, interior lives, or private individual motivations. She also made no effort in the following days, at least so far as her journal reports, to find out any of the information she was lacking, or to speak to the woman who had tried to "give away" her baby to the faeries, or even to record the woman's name. Everything she wrote was filtered through the lens of her own perceptions—we don't know which faeries or liminal beings the woman was attempting to attract (perhaps the konderong, perhaps another sort), nor do we have details of how she was attempting to do it. It is soberingly easy to draw our own conclusions about why she might have tried this—perhaps the woman thought, not unreasonably, that a child stolen by the faeries would have a better life than they would as an enslaved person—but even this is merely a guess, and on some level is disrespectful of the memory of this unnamed woman: She had a complex inner life, and she was making an impossible choice in utterly hellish circumstances. To make definitive conclusions about anyone based on three scanty lines in the journal of an undisciplined secondhand source would be, even in the very, very best-case scenario, lazy scholarship.

AZIZA

By far one of the most benevolent creatures of the American liminal ecology, the aziza are a tiny species that live in anthills or in the bark of certain trees. They are native to West Africa and are now found throughout the South and the Caribbean. They have only one hand and one foot, and they are known for providing all varieties of practical assistance to hunters and people who become lost in the forest. Eliza Berny, who escaped from slavery in 1853 and later became a prolific writer and abolitionist in Connecticut, wrote in her memoirs that during her flight, she and her sister Mary relied on whispering voices in the woods to direct them, especially during cloudy, starless nights or when they were being pursued either by wild animals or by men. The particular details that she provides have led scholars to hypothesize that the Berny sisters were directed by a relay of aziza, as they asked for nothing in return and did not seem to take offense (as many other liminal creatures would have done) when the Berny sisters thanked them and blessed them.

Aziza in modern North America seem to have adapted quite well to a rise in population and suburban sprawl encroaching on their forest habitats, and it is quite common for faerie scholars to collect reports from people who report that, walking alone in the dark, they heard a whisper in the back of their minds that warned them to turn around, or to go back inside, or to run, and that in the cases when they ignored this voice, they encountered without fail something that they would have preferred to avoid, such as dangerous animals, car accidents, or the police.

JUMBEES

The Caribbean jumbee is not, in fact, an independent species, but a hybrid of several transplanted species; this is an unusual phenomenon, and scholars are still not precisely sure why it happened so readily here but not elsewhere in North America or the rest of the world. There are a huge number of extremely localized varieties of jumbee, showing identifiable characteristics of dozens of other species, including those native to Africa, the Americas, Western Europe, and China. Depending on which parent species contributed to the local variety, jumbees span the spectrum of helpful to malignant in their dealings with humans, though like almost all their parent species, they have a tendency to instigate small acts of chaos. Jumbees are classified as a spirit, since they are mostly intangible, though they do have a visible form. Malicious jumbees are easily warded off with the simple, common methods. For instance, a handful of salt, sand, or grain cast on the ground will force them to stop and count the strewn particles; they are incapable of crossing over running water; and they are averse to the sound of bells and the crowing of roosters.

Jumbees are of particular interest to modern scholars who are attempting (unsuccessfully) to map the liminal landscape with more objective, genetic science, as this intense blending of species has been seen nowhere else in the world.

LOA

Some of the most influential and well-documented liminal beings of the American South and the African diaspora are the loa. This is not a singular species, but rather a group of closely related "family" strains (in the same way that a rose faerie and an orchid faerie are both strains of the broader family of flower-faeries, or in the same way that border collies and Great Danes are both dogs). The loa have many shapes, appearances, and natures, which were originally classified by practitioners of Vodun (also known as Vodou in Haiti and Voodoo in Louisiana). These practitioners categorized the loa into families, or nanchons—some kindly and helpful, some aggressive, and some clingy and needy. Family groups share traits amongst their members, and many individual loa have been identified by name. Due to the influence of Catholicism on the original West African Vodun religion, the loa came to be regarded as intermediaries to the spirit world, serving much the same purpose as saints in the Church.

There was a great deal of research and scholarship done on the loa as early as the 1700s and 1800s, and surprisingly a good deal of it is reliable—this is possibly due to the fact that the loa were well known to be difficult to work with and potentially dangerous (including the possibility of an opportunistic loa "riding" or possessing a human host). This led early (note: almost universally white) scholars to take great precaution and rely mostly on the reports and guidance of expert practitioners.

THE PETRO LOA

The Petro are a family of loa that emerged in Haiti, born from the unimaginable rage and despair of the enslaved peoples, the Petro are ferocious, quick to anger and vicious in their vengeance. This family (of which the loa Ezili Dantor is the matriarch) shares a taste for percussion music and gunpowder. Much like the Unseelie Court of the European fae, the Petro and their motivations are often interpreted by humans as "evil." In fact, when approached with humble respect, the Petro are as willing to provide supernatural assistance with righteous tasks as they are with malicious ones, though their great strength lies in undertakings that require hot tempers, fierce spirits, and deep fury.

Conservation Across the Four Domains

The "four domains" refers to the elemental classification of liminal beings—earth, air, fire, and water—which, while poetic, is now considered to be somewhat simplistic and antiquated. Under this system, tree spirits like dryads were classified in the earth domain alongside underground dwellers like cave trolls, though they bear no resemblance and occupy wildly different niches within the ecosystem. Likewise, ether sprites are classified in the air domain, though historically their main source of nourishment was vents from underground pools of natural gas. So are they truly of the air domain, or does earth make more sense? Or fire, as the gas is flammable? And what of beings like selkies, which can transition between the ocean and land—are they in the water domain or the earth domain? All of this is mere quibbling, and has mostly been disregarded by all but the most traditional and pedantic of scholars.

Regardless of domains and classifications, by far the biggest threat to life as we know it—both the liminal and the mundane—are climate change and other symptoms of human impact on the environment. We have already driven many species to extinction, many more are on the verge of collapse, and yet some have found opportunities to thrive as a direct result of the damage to the environment.

ETHER SPRITES

Ether sprites were once believed to be the messengers of the gods, bringing prophecies and visions to certain favored humans. Modern science has provided a much more rational explanation: The visions came from deposits of natural gas, which, leaching from the ground to be inhaled by unknowing passersby, caused symptoms such as hallucinations, light-headedness, or a disconnected dreamlike state (think of legends of the Oracle of Delphi, for example). As natural gas is also the ether sprites' primary food source, they often congregate in areas where it is plentiful and naturally occurring. The erroneous conclusion that the sprites were bringing visions and messages was a classic premodern case of mistaking correlation for causation.

In the urban environment, ether sprites pose an irritating problem—they are most commonly found around gas stations and, as they require no oxygen or sunlight to survive, an infestation in a station's underground tanks can swiftly grow to an unmanageable size and cause catastrophic financial losses.

There are some scholars who theorize that ether sprites could be used for a variety of useful tasks—detecting the presence of radon gas in basements, clearing carbon monoxide and other dangerous gases from difficult-to-ventilate areas, or cleaning airborne pollution from the world's smoggiest cities. But all of these items share a persistent core problem, which is that ether sprites are almost impossible to keep in captivity, and completely impossible to both keep and use profitably. One can be captured in an airtight tank, and that does well enough for study, but then of course there is no easy way to allow it access to the gases that it needs to consume. Any crack or hole in the tank is enough for the sprite to escape.

Ether sprites can be difficult to spot, but they are easily distinguished from other species by their almost transparent, iridescent coloration and the unique shape of their wings. Although they congregate, sometimes in great numbers, around concentrated sources of their food, they do not live in any kind of organized colony, as pixies do, nor do they build nests of any kind. Instead, ether sprites lay egg sacs in sheltered spots, usually low to the ground, such as in the twisted roots of trees, on the undersides of abandoned cars, or in difficult-to-access nooks of architecture. Like brownies, they are one of the supernatural species that have most thrived in modern, urban environments, though I suspect that if the use of clean energy continues to grow more widespread, we may see the ether sprites' population numbers drop back to what they must have been like in the pre-industrial era.

While ether sprites are harmless to humans and animals, scholars recommend looking for them in their "wild" habitat (inasmuch as gas stations and drilling sites can be considered wild), rather than attempting to attract them to a specific location. (I will remind readers that although allowing a tank of propane to gently leak might be an effective "birdfeeder" to entice them, it is also a very dangerous one. I firmly recommend against doing this.)

CAVE TROLLS AND OTHER UNDERGROUND SPECIES

Underground-dwelling and earth-associated creatures are famously resistant to the effects of iron, so the first subterranean mass-transit systems (including train tunnels bored through mountains and the Metropolitan Railway, the precursor to the modern London Underground) faced the challenges of managing infestations alongside the more mundane issues of flooding, cave-ins, and ventilation—all of which, of course, could be exacerbated by inhabitants of the earth that they were boring through. Maintaining a good relationship with a colony of knockers, for example (a variety of underground-dwelling creatures known for their distinctive tapping through the walls of rock that miners were working on), meant that miners sometimes received advance warning about incipient dangers. A threatened or alienated colony, on the other hand, could cause those same catastrophes. And, of course, like most fae creatures, knockers and other underground species do not share a human concept of morality, as both friendly and unfriendly colonies were well known to engage in mischief and minor pranks.

In hindsight it seems like it should have been obvious that the installation of the rails would have little effect on the trolls, knockers, and rock-eaters. They are creatures of the earth, and iron is merely refined earth, and steel is merely refined iron mixed with carbon (a different variety of earth). It was only because the first architects were drawing on the expertise of miners—who in the early Industrial Revolution were viewed as being incredibly superstitious (though for the most part they were just *correct*)—to deal with the creatures using their own tried-and-true methods. These involved both leaving offerings of beer and tobacco in the hopes of appeasing the creatures, and using various methods to drive them out.

The first technological development that drastically reduced the issues facing underground construction was the use of dynamite to assist in excavation—for years, miners had used musket shots and small fireworks to scare off the infesting creatures. Dynamite worked thrice as well, for the same reason that loud explosions work to drive off bats and some varieties of birds from an area. Earth dwellers communicate and find their way by sensing vibrations through the ground, and scholars suspect now that they may be particularly sensitive to feeling the ground damaged. On a smaller scale (such as a person digging a hole to bury a body or hide treasure, a farmer plowing a field, a miner with an old-fashioned pickax, etc.), they are drawn closer out of curiosity, but larger, louder disturbances are intolerable—this probably serves the obvious evolutionary advantage of helping them avoid predators bigger than they are, but researchers have also noticed that in the wake of a lightning strike, earth dwellers give a wide berth to the area for days, and sometimes weeks.

This brings us to the second technological development, and the more dramatic of the two: the use of electricity to power underground transit. The first electrified urban rail, the City and South

London Railway, which opened in 1890, effectively ended the problem of managing infestations of earth dwellers. The later proliferation of buried electrical lines in most of the world's cities means that trolls and knockers are all but unknown in the modern urban environment.

ROCK-EATERS

Thought to be a species related to trolls, rock-eaters are found throughout Northern Europe and Greenland. They show little sign of measurable intelligence. Rock-eaters live exclusively underground and have craggy, grayish skin and no eyes—they are thought to navigate by vibrations or possibly by some kind of echolocation using liminal energies. Their most distinguishing features are their broad mouths, strong jaws, and flat teeth, with which they chew their way through the earth and crush rocks into gravel. Like rabbits, rock-eaters' teeth grow continuously and at a fast rate. If kept from adequately rough food for even a couple weeks, their teeth can quickly grow out of control and prevent them from eating anything at all, resulting in death by starvation.

RIVER SPIRITS

For as long as humans have been exerting their will on the environments around them, the liminal world has been reacting in kind, and not always cooperatively. Scottish folklore provides the story of St. Winning and the River Garnock: The saint and his companions were fishing in the river one day and caught nothing; in revenge, St. Winning cursed the river so that it would never have any fish. In response, the river simply shifted its course and thereby avoided the curse. The River Garnock, located in Ayrshire, did indeed change course over a few hundred years, and though we have no conclusive proof as to whether St. Winning was a real person, or whether he actually laid a curse on the river, it does form the beginnings of a pattern.

River spirits have always been particularly resilient against human interference. Water always takes the path of least resistance, and if an obstacle is put in its place, then it will merely find a way to go around, even if that takes a few hundred years. Likewise, water spirits and faeries have always had an aggressive reaction to any attempt to dam their rivers; the hostility of their response has only increased alongside the scale and technological grandeur of humanity's structures. For instance, in pre-industrial times, a team of dam builders might expect to encounter misfortunes and minor acts of sabotage, but compare that to the death toll recorded during the building of the Hoover Dam. During the construction of the dam, nearly a hundred deaths were deemed to be accidental, while several more were attributed to "suicide," most tellingly, the drowning of the project's two original geological surveyors, J. G. Tierney and Harold Connelly. Yet once the building of the dam actually commenced, its construction workers inadvertently benefited from their use of technology in several ways. First, the use of dynamite to blast away the loose rock of the canyon walls served as a short-term repellent for supernatural beings inhabiting the area. (Using loud noises and explosions as a method of scaring off spirits is well documented in several folkloric traditions of the world.) Second, the extensive use of grout-filled steel pipes running through the concrete of the dam served as an active deterrent to the spirits who, returning after the dynamite blasts had ceased, might have otherwise had the strength to cause more damage during the building process.

EAST ASIAN DRAGONS

East Asian dragons have a strong sympathetic connection with water, particularly rivers. They are a localized elemental creature, which means that they do not follow the movements and migrations of humans, but instead maintain a connection to a single body of water for the span of their lifetime, which can be thousands of years long, provided they are not killed. Pollution of rivers and other harmful human influences can disturb the dragons (though they are generally benevolent and slow to anger), causing them to bring excessive rain, thunderstorms, and flooding to surrounding areas.

In the nineteenth century, Western scholars first tried to discredit and deny the existence of East Asian dragons, then attempted to use proven sightings of them to support the theory that European dragons must have once lived and had since gone extinct, using dinosaur fossils as the other pillar of that latter argument. We now know both of these claims to be conclusively false—first, because the dozens of species of East Asian dragons compose a unique evolutionary family that has already been well documented by hundreds of years of scholars; and second, that sometimes dinosaur fossils are just dinosaur fossils.

These dragons are exclusive to East Asia, as the farthest west one has been documented is in Mongolia's Lake Khuvsgul.

CORRELATION vs. CAUSATION:
HURRICANES AND FAERIES OF THE TEMPESTS

Scholars and poets have long known of the association between certain liminal beings and severe weather events. One of the most famous faeries in fiction, Ariel from Shakespeare's *The Tempest*, causes a great storm at the beginning of the play, an act that scholars with a more historical bent cite as evidence that Tudor England clearly believed in the "causation" theory of faerie interaction with the weather. However, as in all historical matters, the truth is more complex than that—people have always had a variety of different theories and opinions on all scientific matters throughout history. There has never been a pure and perfect consensus.

Even today, the "causation" theory (the idea that certain beings have the ability to generate storms from nothing) holds firm in certain segments of the field, but while there are a slight few beings that have been clearly documented as having such powers (the psonen of North America and the dragons of China, for example), the "correlation" theory (the idea that some liminal beings are attracted to storms and severe weather events, or perhaps to the conditions that result from those storms) is, in general, the more popular one. There is also a theory popular with a small percentage of scholars that is fondly known as "corsation," hypothesizing that weather faeries can subtly and inadvertently influence atmospheric conditions (e.g., barometric pressure, wind strength) that then go on to cause storms as a side effect.

Whatever the truth is, whether there is an overarching pattern or not, over the past twenty years, significant changes have been documented amongst air-aligned creatures, particularly those associated with weather events. Due to climate change, scientists have noted that hurricanes and typhoons are becoming more severe, with stronger winds and greater amounts of precipitation. Likewise, scholars of the fae have noted through field observation (often at great personal danger to themselves) an increase of as much as 10 percent in the amount of wind sprites spotted during hurricanes, as well as noting that individual creatures are, on average, growing larger—up to the size of a crow, rather than the sprites of thirty years ago that were recorded and photographed as being roughly wren-sized.

DESERTiFICATION

As climate change progresses and few truly impactful solutions are implemented to curtail it, desertification has progressed as a side effect, creating wider dead zones where liminal beings and mundane ones have a difficult time both living and adapting. Not all species will be completely endangered, of course—there are many that thrive in near-barren, hot climates, such as the Middle Eastern djinn. However, even desert ecologies will be adversely affected by climate change—most deserts are not wholly empty of life, after all, and extreme heat, extended drought, and wildfires will kill off even the hardiest flora and fauna.

One of the species likely to be amongst the first to suffer the effects of climate change is the Mongolian death worm, a creature about the length and width of a person's arm with the ability to give a fatal electric shock to anything that touches it. The death worm's native habitat, the Gobi Desert, experiences great extremes of temperatures, often with quite rapid changes occurring within a single day, but the creature itself is rarely seen during summer daylight hours, hiding in underground tunnels until the sun sets and temperatures drop.

THE ROC

Hunted to extinction in the 1400s, rocs were a species of giant bird, said to be big enough to black out the sun when one passed overhead. Rocs dwelled mostly in deserts and remote, inaccessible mountain regions, and based on historical accounts and the scanty amount of physical remains found, scholars suspect that, like an albatross, the roc could stay airborne for weeks, possibly months, at a time.

The roc is one of the first liminal creatures we know of to go extinct because of human activity. The last of them, the Great Roc of Petra, was killed in the autumn of 1473 by Prince Hilāl ibn Khalis, whose court poet Zuhayr al-Ashtar later composed a piece about the event. The poem, at once a viscerally poignant eulogy, a scathing critique of the prince, and a diatribe against mankind's compulsion to destroy nature's magnificent wildness, so offended the prince that he had the poet stripped naked and driven out of the city and nearly every copy of the poem burned. It was only rediscovered in 2005, with an English translation published the following year by Dr. Yasmine Moss:

> The greatest crime of all must be the thirst for destruction:
> Allah, once I stood at the ruins of beauty,
> I saw your vast glory lying dead on the rocks and sand,
> Its wings stretched from horizon to horizon,
> From my feet, a river of tears flowed that far as well . . .
> —from "The Death of Beauty," Zuhayr al-Ashtar (1443–1475)

DRYADS

It is a common misconception that dryads come in singular entities. Traditionally, a dryad has been described simply as "a tree spirit" or "a faerie that resides in a plant or has an existential connection to a plant" (some flower-faeries have been historically classified as dryads). Dryads often appear vaguely female and usually display physical attributes of the species of tree that they are connected to. However, we know now that talking about or studying a single dryad is about as useful as talking about a single bee or a single ant: It is much more useful and scientifically relevant to study the entire colony. With dryads, that means the whole forest.

When a single tree is felled in a forest, either by human activity or by natural forces such as strong winds or lightning, the liminal ecology is not significantly affected. The dryad colony, overlaying the forest, works around the injury until the forest heals itself. However, in cases of widespread and systematic deforestation, there is no opportunity for this to happen—dryads move from tree to tree, becoming condensed into smaller and smaller areas, and sometimes two colonies are gradually driven together. This results in illness or uncharacteristic violence, both within and between colonies. Trees that do grow back are scantier and less healthy, and this has a domino effect that impacts the entire food chain of the forest.

Tree farms appear to be one of the easiest solutions to this problem, but, like corporations running monocrop megafarms, these often create a dead zone for liminal creatures, who seem to thrive most in areas of biodiversity (see, for example, the Amazon rainforest, which has such a wealth of species, both mundane and liminal, that we are still discovering hundreds of new species every year). Replanting efforts have helped some, but as it can take twenty to thirty years for a tree to mature enough to be capable of hosting one or more dryads, this is also an imperfect solution. Currently, the best option available (in terms of immediate impact and positive effects) is to designate more forested wildernesses as protected areas, but since there is often such a resistance to expanding protected areas within the government and corporate lobbying interests, this, too, is a frustratingly imperfect solution.

BEASTS OF THE
AMAZON RAINFOREST

As mind-bogglingly rich in mundane biodiversity as the Amazon is, it is equally rich in liminal biodiversity. The rainforest contains tens of thousands of sprite-like species alone, some as small as mosquitoes. Some mundane species are so extraordinary that they were originally considered to be fae in origin, and some liminal beings appear so ordinary that they have actually been captured and assigned scientific classification by ordinary biologists.

However, more intelligent creatures also abound: On the more dangerous end of the spectrum is the mapinguari, a creature reported to be markedly taller than the average adult human and strongly resembling a giant sloth. Like a threatened skunk, it exudes a dire odor that is capable of knocking hunters unconscious if they inhale too much of it. The mapinguari is carnivorous, possessing a gaping, ravenous maw in the center of its stomach, though it generally prefers to attack livestock rather than more dangerous prey.

On the less dreadful end of the spectrum is the Mayantu, a tree-dwelling species, roughly humanoid but possessing the face of a frog or a toad. Like many fae creatures, they are quite territorial. They operate by the standard guidelines of faerie morality: If you treat them with politeness and respect, their benevolence abounds, and they have been known to cure diseases and rescue those who require aid. However, violation of the laws of hospitality (in this case, causing harm to the forest or its inhabitants) will anger the Mayantu, who will revoke their aid and sometimes torment their targets with confusion.

MERROWS, SIRENS, SELKIES, AND COASTAL POLLUTION

The liminal beings of the rivers and oceans have always operated at a remove from humans and their civilization. While many of the creatures listed in this book live in response to or as reflections of human society, ocean dwellers act instead as avatars of all that is yet unknown and alien. In some species, it is easy to identify sentience—the selkies of the northern coasts of the British Isles, for example, are known in folklore to shed their seal skins and walk amongst people undetected (one of the only liminal beings to do such a thing without a motive that involves seduction, kidnapping, or murder), and the blubber-insulated merrows of the polar region bear a great deal of similarity to whales and dolphins in the sophistication of their language. In other species, certain mimicking behaviors may suggest a human-like intelligence, but only at the viewer's, or listener's, peril. The beguiling song of the sirens sounds much like a human's—a similar luring technique as that used by mundane animals of the African savannah and jungle, which are able to mimic a human child's cry accurately enough to draw the unwary away from their campfires.

And there are creatures of the sea—dozens, if not hundreds or thousands—which show no sign of human-like intelligence at all:

those gaunt horrors of the deepest parts of the ocean with bulging eyes and bioluminescent lights like the anglerfish, the great kraken, the sea serpents, and the shipbreaker-spirits that fly through the water like manta rays. Humanity faces the very real possibility that there are some species we have already destroyed without ever once encountering them.

EL NADDAHA

El Naddaha is a species of siren found exclusively in Egypt's Nile River. Like many other species in this family, El Naddaha appears as a beautiful human woman with long hair and a lovely voice, who calls young men to the river and (presumably) drowns them. Sightings of El Naddaha in the historical record are exceptionally scanty, and the species was only documented regularly beginning in the mid-1900s. Scholars now suspect that the damming of the Nile (the Aswan Low Dam in 1902, followed by the Aswan High Dam in the 1960s) and the subsequent regulation of the annual floods was a key factor in creating a stable environment for El Naddaha to flourish.

MERROWS

Bearing the proper name for the creature that is often erroneously called a "mermaid," these sea dwellers have been wildly miscategorized for centuries. To start with, they are not half fish—they are mammals. Scholars disagree as to whether they should be grouped together with cetaceans (whales, dolphins), pinnipeds (seals, walruses), or the scientific order Sirenia (manatees, dugongs), because all three groups are represented somewhere in the sheer variety of the different localized types of merrows—deep-sea merrows are more whale-like, northern coastal merrows more seal-like, temperate merrows more manatee-like. Regardless of localization, while most depictions of "mermaids" present them as lithe, pretty maidens, merrows (like all water-dwelling mammals) are insulated by a layer of blubber that helps preserve body heat even in warm-water tropical regions. Merrows bear only a passing resemblance to humans; though they do possess forelimbs, their "hands" are merely divided fins that are about as useful as a thickly mittened human hand.

There is only one known species of merrow that has the ability to transition between both freshwater and saltwater: the African jengu, which is found in rivers and along the coast of the Bight of Biafra. Miengu (plural of jengu) are known for their characteristic gap teeth, which are considered very beautiful, as well as for their powers to cure diseases and bring luck—miengu are one of the more actively benevolent species of merrow.

OIL SPILLS

Oil spills at sea (such as the *Exxon Valdez* spill in 1989, or the *Deepwater Horizon* oil spill in 2010) cause a nigh-incalculable amount of damage to the environment, but the effect on the liminal ecology is somewhat more complex. While we unquestionably see an overwhelmingly negative impact on the vast majority of species, there are several that seem uniquely suited to thrive in such a catastrophe.

Oil is a material accessible to both fire- and earth-aligned beings, which means that the vast majority of species for whom it could be a source of nourishment find it inaccessible when it is floating out at sea. Once it washes up on shore (having already done immense damage to the 99 percent of the environment it doesn't benefit), it attracts several species of grime-eaters and occasionally trolls. Scholars initially thought that these creatures could be used to help with cleanup efforts, but earth-aligned species tend to have extremely slow metabolisms, so although they flock to oil-devastated shorelines in great numbers, it would take dozens of years of their steady presence for significant improvements to be seen, during which time the severely negative effects on the rest of the local environment would continue apace. Most fire-aligned species (such as hearth-salamanders), on the other hand, are seen aboveground as rarely as anglerfish are seen in shallow waters, so while they do consume oil at a greater rate, there simply aren't enough of them to be useful—and moreover, fire-aligned species are often highly volatile. A startled salamander could potentially cause more harm than good by lighting a fire in self-defense—besides the oil releasing vast amounts of harmful burn-off into the air, a fire on shore can spread, destroying property or starting uncontrollable wildfires.

GARBAGE- AND GRIME-EATERS

Another example of liminal creatures who have benefited from (or, perhaps more accurately, adapted to exploit) modern human life are the grime-eaters, a category that includes goblins and goblin variants, the Sewer Blob of North Carolina, the Japanese akaname (a yōkai that is known for licking filth out of bathrooms), the gulon of Scandinavia (a gluttonous carrion-eater), and the vodyanoy of Russia (a frog-like water spirit that has adapted enthusiastically toward sewers and drainpipes as a habitat).

With the great abundance of trash piling up in landfills (and waste in sewage treatment plants), we have created for these beings a habitat of plentiful food and safety from predators, so population numbers amongst the grime-eaters have been growing steadily. While a very few are helpful, consuming garbage and filth and rendering it down quickly into biodegradable waste, and some are mostly harmless (such as the akaname—it has a very frightening appearance with its greenish skin and creepily long tongue, but it is generally unconcerned with humans), most species of this category are at least semi-violent toward humans.

One of humanity's greatest dumping grounds is, of course, the ocean. In the middle of the Pacific, the Great Garbage Patch covers 1.6 million square kilometers, an area more than twice the size of Texas, in which scholars have documented the beginnings of adaptations amongst the liminal creatures who live in or near it, some of them very similar to the mutations of the faeries in Chernobyl (see page 161). Sprites and lesser water-aligned faeries are showing physiological changes that somehow may help them make plastic waste a form of accessible nutrition. Other changes are behavioral: Merrow of this region of the ocean have developed different eating habits, biting off pieces of fish and birds that they catch rather than consuming them whole, probably in order to avoid intaking any microplastics or plastic shards that those animals themselves have eaten. While this seems to be an effective survival tactic for the merrows so far, it means that they have to kill more prey in order to get adequate sustenance, which may have long-term devastating effects on the population of fish and birds, and result in a cascading effect down the food chain.

AKANAME,
THE BATHROOM-LICKER

The akaname were most famously documented by the scholar and artist Toriyama Sekien in his 1776 book *The Illustrated Night Parade of a Hundred Demons* (画図百鬼夜行, *Gazu Hyakki Yagyō*; an encyclopedia or field guide very similar to this one, and the first of four wildly popular volumes that Toriyama published on the subject). The akaname is a yōkai that, as the name suggests, inhabits bathrooms and feeds on the filth that collects in poorly cleaned tubs and toilets—mold, soap scum, dirt, and human waste. Just as people used to believe that maggots spawned directly from rotting meat, the akaname actually does spontaneously self-generate in these filthy, humid environments. The akaname is about the size of a child, with a long red tongue and greenish skin. Most varieties have a foot with only one long, clawed toe.

THE FAER!ES OF CHERNOBYL

There are certain concepts and occurrences that are most easily explained and understood by starting with the digestible structure of a fairy tale: Once upon a time, there was a castle that was warded by magic. Whenever a traveler attempted to approach, they would find the path twisting away under their feet, leading them away from the castle instead of toward it. It was only through great effort that a traveler could pass across the wards' fields, and once they had, it was almost impossible to escape again.

Scholars do not have accurate and reliable maps of the ley lines of Eastern Europe before 1986, particularly not the smaller paths and their fractals. Though those interested can take the inaccurate, incomplete, and imprecise maps to be a rough estimation, even without them one can conclude that before the Chernobyl disaster, the ley lines were *dramatically* different in location, direction, and quantity than they are today.

The first scientifically rigorous map of Ukraine's ley lines was produced in 2002 by amateur cartographer Taras Ivanov, and it throws the radioactive blight on the landscape into sharp perspective. Extending far outside the thirty-kilometer exclusion zone is a toroid of distorted fractals, a great circle of blurred and confused lines around the site of the disaster, intersecting at strange angles and bearing no logical flow of power from one point to another. Ley lines are often described as a railroad network of energy, but in this instance, it is easier to picture them as rivers, and to imagine the toroid around Chernobyl as a swamp where the water stands stagnant. Like the wards around the castle in the fairy tale, the confusion of the lines makes it difficult for fae creatures (or those carrying magical items, or the particularly sensitive) to cross through the toroid. They may find themselves lost, or misdirected, or turned back the way they came. And, like in the fairy tale, any supernatural creature that does manage to push through to the center would find it impossible to come back out, much like crossing the event horizon of a black hole. Beyond that event horizon, in the center of the toroid, is Chernobyl itself, which is not so much crossed by ley lines as it is a well of power that would be incandescent were it visible to the human eye.

Besides the effects on the physical environment, this distortion of energy and power has had profound effects on the species living in the area as well. Amongst mundane animals, the rates of mutation are much lower than were originally expected, disregarding the large spike in radioactivity-caused mutation within the first six months after the disaster. However, even decades afterward, faeries and other liminal creatures of the area still show strong evidence of the effects of the fallout. In some cases, it has made their innate powers stronger and wilder; in others it has caused distortion of physical features and a greater amount of variance within individual species. The common European faerie appears across the continent in variations that will camouflage them in their local environment by matching their bodies to the colors of bark or their wings to the shape, size, and appearance of leaves of the prevailing species of tree. Inside the Chernobyl toroid, however, there are variations that include strange, unnatural colors (rust, red, or purple), or spines like pine needles growing from their flesh. The faeries of Chernobyl also tend to be larger than their counterparts elsewhere.

The only other nuclear disaster that has even come close to approaching the scale of Chernobyl was the Fukushima Daiichi nuclear disaster in 2011, but experts have estimated that the damage there was only a tenth of that caused during the earlier catastrophe. While scholars have noticed some distortion of ley lines around Fukushima (though not nearly so severe as those making up the Chernobyl toroid), it has been difficult to determine whether local fae (e.g., yōsei, kappa, tengu) have exhibited any signs of mutation, mostly due to those species' tendencies toward elusiveness making them harder to locate and document.

It is worth noting, also, that no distortion toroid exists around Hiroshima, Nagasaki, or any of the test sites of the atomic bomb, leading many to conclude that the distortions must be linked somehow to the specific radioactive isotopes released at the site of the disasters (cesium at Chernobyl and Fukushima, versus uranium in the bombs).

Safe Hunts for the Beginning Fae-Spotter

There is always some degree of risk associated with exploration, whether from wildlife (either mundane or supernatural), difficult terrain, or personal error. While many of the fae creatures mentioned in this book are aggressive (or intelligent enough to be intentionally malicious), scholars have still made dedicated and ongoing attempts to study them. It is only through educating ourselves about our surrounding environments, both natural and social, that we have the practical knowledge of how to protect and cultivate them so that they may thrive—or, in cases where great damage has been done, begin the slow process of recovery and reclamation.

The following section lists three types of liminal being which most experts agree are as low-risk as one can expect to find, appropriate for those who are just setting out on this journey. This does not necessarily mean that these hunts are entirely risk-*free*—even amateur ornithologists (of the mundane sort) face risks, though birdwatching is generally considered to be a relaxing and low-stress hobby: sunburn, sprained ankles, territorial wildlife, bird droppings right down the back of one's best sweater, and so on. Please do your research in advance, honor any prohibitions of the area in which you are searching, take a guide familiar with the area whenever possible, use all appropriate safety precautions including your common sense, do not allow children to explore unsupervised, and be very careful not to behave destructively toward the natural environment in a search for the supernatural.

The Lesser Flower-Faerie

Flower-faeries are categorized in the broad spectrum of plant-associated beings, such as dryads—and indeed, as mentioned previously in this book, some dryads were formerly categorized as variations on flower-faeries. This discussion of taxonomies could get very complicated and boring (especially for beginners), so let us consider them through the metaphor of fish: Dryads are tuna; lesser flower-faeries are minnows.

The lesser flower-faeries, which comprise thousands and thousands of different types, are each closely associated with a particular flower, shrub, fungus, or other small plant: roses, dandelions, daisies, mushrooms . . . Even herbs such as thyme, rosemary, and lavender attract flower-faeries. Each faerie has physical traits that echo their associated plants—size; coloration and shape of the flowers, leaves, and stems; seasonality; and so on.

Flower-faeries are not a higher-order being, which means they do not have the intelligence to be malicious, but they do have natural weapons—teeth and sometimes claws, stingers, or thorns—and some varieties are territorial. Just as an agitated wren could fly in your face and leave you scratched and a bit shaken up, so, too, do flower-faeries have the ability to defend themselves if necessary. They won't be able to kill you, but they might be able to give you an unpleasant few moments or injure you, especially if they attack your face and eyes. To reduce this risk, take care not to harass them, just as you would for any other wild creature, and wear a sturdy jacket and glasses or safety goggles. Do your best to identify toxic plants in the area, and if you see a faerie associated with one, avoid it—a poison ivy, poison oak, or poison sumac faerie will without question provide you a very . . . *particular and memorable* sort of learning experience, but it's not going to be a fun time.

If you do not have an established flower garden of your own, local public parks or botanical gardens are another fine option for a hunt. Flower-faeries tend to avoid highly trafficked areas and neatly manicured plots, so look instead for areas of the gardens which have grown (or, better yet, overgrown) in a natural sort of way. If you do not have access to a botanical garden near you, do not lose hope! Flower-faeries can sometimes be spotted even in weedy, neglected window boxes in the middle of a busy city or a forgotten planter pot by the porch steps.

Note: Do your best to keep domestic pets, particularly cats, away from these planters and window boxes. Cats can see liminal beings better than nearly any other mundane creature and are arguably semi-liminal beings themselves, but flower-faeries are small, fluttery things, and cats like to eat them.

The Common American
Ghost-light

Ghost-lights are one of the widest-spread families of liminal beings, so much so that they constitute an entire scientific genus of their own (*ignis fatuus*). The world over, they share notable characteristics, though they naturally vary from region to region, as local cultures have adapted their beliefs about what they mean. The common American ghost-light is as similar to its European cousin, the will-o'-the-wisp, as the American wren is to the European wren. Ghost-lights are a familiar sight for even hobbyist fae-spotters and are one of the safest for beginners to search for, provided they use common sense and take the appropriate necessary precautions when dealing with potential dangers of the mundane world (wildlife, disorienting landscape, weather, etc.).

Ghost-lights appear in marshes and other wetlands as small, glowing balls of light that float above the ground, sometimes only a few inches, sometimes several feet. They are thought to be produced by the decaying corpses of people who became lost and drowned in swamps, marshes, and wetlands. In some locations, ghost-lights stay quite still; in others they are known to drift about. This behavior often lures the over-curious and under-cautious into the swamps, where they become lost and/or drown, but it is imperative to note that scholars have proven *several* times now that such accidents are *not* caused by malice of the ghost-lights themselves, which seem to show no intelligence at all.

Ghost-lights span the globe. In Mexico, they are known as *luces del tesoro* and often appear near ancient burial grounds, archaeological digs, and hidden caches of money. Through the southern end of South America, they are called *luz mala*. In Abenaki lore, ghost-lights are called *chibaiskweda*; in Louisiana, *feu-follet*; in Bangladesh, *aleya*; in Japan, *hitodama*; in Finland, *aarnivalkea*; in Australia, the Min Min light; in Norway, the Hessdalen lights. While there are some legends that do ascribe malicious natures to the ghost-lights, claiming that they steal children or consume the souls of the unwary, again scholars have proven conclusively that ghost-lights are not capable of ill intent. Accidents happen in relation to them because people are foolish, unprepared, or conclude that simply because the ghost-lights are quite safe, the rest of the swamp would be, too, and therefore disregard the natural, mundane dangers of snakes, alligators, geese, and coyotes.

As mentioned above, ghost-lights are a great first hunt for the beginning fae-spotter. When preparing for a hunt, remember that many wetlands are federally protected areas and off-limits to the public. However, many national parks also have hiking or canoeing trails, some designed to be a journey of several days, which is ideal. Time a hunt as close to the new moon as possible: Darker nights make faint ghost-lights easier to see. Many hobbyists believe that ghost-lights appear more frequently deeper into the wetlands, but the rate of appearances has no statistical significance based on location, and most stories that we have about ghost-lights concern people noticing them as they pass along the *edges* of a swamp. There is no need to go deep into the area, particularly if you are inexperienced or feel ill at ease for any reason.

AWES-KON-WA

Named by the Abenaki of the northeastern United States and Eastern Canada, this native species is often mistaken for a small brown wren. It can be found in mature conifer forests in Eastern and Central Canada and New England during the spring and summer, and throughout the Eastern Seaboard, the Southeast, and parts of the Midwest during the winter. Like the Luck Pigeon, it can be difficult to distinguish an awes-kon-wa from a mundane wren, but the former has a few distinctive features. It has slightly lighter, glossy (almost glittering) coloring and a unique song; they are also more sensitive to disturbances of the forest than mundane wrens are, so forests that are too closely managed or too popular with hikers may be difficult places to spot them. The awes-kon-wa is cautious of humans and has extremely limited supernatural powers, though it has been known to heal minor wounds if the person observing it can lure it close enough with a nonthreatening demeanor and food. It is not a mischief-causing species, and anyone with a pair of binoculars, a backpack full of patience, and the knowledge of basic ornithology should be able to make a few possible identifications.

Afterword

And what of the faeries we haven't even begun to conceive of yet? What of all the in-between spaces of the universe we haven't yet passed through? If one day we manage to leave our planet in any kind of significant numbers, will we find tommyknockers on Mars? Spirits beyond our comprehension in the interstellar void?

Or will we bring our faeries with us when we venture out from this planetary Old World to a truly New one? Is there some far-distant future where we will have built a way station between the stars through which a constant stream of travelers flow on their way from one place to another, and when we reach that crossroads will we still find a Gentleman there, waiting for us, offering us a bargain: "What will you give in exchange for your heart's desire?"

Acknowledgments

I t always such a humbling sort of joy to write this part, to look back on all the people who are responsible, in part, for helping bring the book into the world. Considering the short length of this one, there was a disproportionately high number of helpers!

First and foremost, of course, the team at Tiller Press! Ronnie Alvarado and Michael Anderson were such a delight to work with, and Kate Davids is a downright superhero of research. I was also thrilled to be able to work with Miles Äijälä, the illustrator—I've known Miles for years and have always been blown away by his art, so it was a true honor to partner with him on this book.

I owe a huge, huge hug to Navah Wolfe, who put my name forward for this project—I really can't thank you enough, Navah! My agent, Britt Siess, has been a wonderful partner and an incredibly graceful diplomat; I hope we have many more years of working together! Thank you also to Joy Demorra, who told me about Scottish fairytales; Jennifer Mace, who suggested The Pigeon; Martin Cahill, who asked for dryads; Sarah Guan, who took me out for amazing Chinese food and told me about the jiāngshī; Amy Hahn and Jean Blakeman, who once or twice did what they could to give me a few more hours in the week; Saint Gibson and Kit Mayquist, who told me about the huldufólk . . . The list could go on for days, quite frankly.

And as always, my heart's gratitude to those who have supported me in other, more abstract ways: the Serpentcast Discord chat room and my Patreon supporters, for an astounding amount of love and generosity and community spirit; the Sack, who are the best collection of writer-friends, colleagues, and all-around good eggs that I could ask for, not to mention objectionably talented; and the D.S. & T.B. Appreciation Society, who know what they did and are so spoilt (and much beloved).

But of the people that I need to recognize as part of the making of this book, there is another which cannot go unsaid.

I wrote this book at my home in Western Massachusetts, the traditional ancestral homeland of the Nipmuc and Pocumtuc First Nations. It is of vital importance to understand and acknowledge that the occupation of these lands was done through great and ongoing acts of violence, and to erase that history perpetuates that violence and carries it into the future. I cannot simply refuse to participate in this, because by my very position in society, I am a member of the occupying force and have benefited (and will continue to benefit) from the structural oppression of these and other marginalized communities. I cannot ever fully opt out of these benefits; I can only choose, again and again, which side of the fight I'd like to be on.

So you may ask: What does this have to do with this book in particular? What does it have to do with faeries or any other magical beings for that matter?

When I was first asked to write this book, the Tiller Press team and I discussed what sort of angle I would take on it. We knew we wanted something very modern, something that was serious and meaningful, something about the ways in which human behavior has changed and impacted the lives of the wildlife around us: We're facing the ever-more-real certainty of cataclysmic climate change in our near future, but in our present, we have already destroyed or irreparably damaged huge amounts of our global environment and driven many species to endangerment or extinction.

But as I started actually writing the book, I realized very quickly that this exclusively ecological perspective was simply not enough. If I was to write a book about the impact of people on the natural environment, there was a huge, huge issue that could not be ignored.

The argument I have posited in this book is that supernatural beings are tied either to the land itself or to the people living on the land. This reflects the beliefs of peoples all across the world: Some spirits are tied to a place—a certain forest, pond, or mountain—and some are carried with us like invisible luggage. America's history over the last five hundred years is built of stratified layers of violence against many of its peoples: against the indigenous peoples who first lived here; against the Africans who were brought here against their will and enslaved by white landowners; against the Chinese laborers who built the railroad systems throughout the west; against the communities of immigrants and refugees, "the huddled masses yearning to breathe free"; against the generations of all of those people who have been born here and who died here, all of whom were told a pretty lie about the promise of America and were then comprehensively exploited for profit. All of these people carried their physical belongings on their backs and their spiritual belongings in their hearts and souls. To exploit or appropriate these beliefs—using inappropriately what does not culturally belong to me—would be to add another thin layer of violence. But, on the other hand, to ignore or erase them would be a serious violence as well.

I spent a long time thinking seriously about how to navigate between these two paths, I discussed it with people whose opinion I trusted, I researched. I am uncertain, even now with the book already written, whether it is possible to thread the eye of this needle with the appropriate amount of respect and grace that it deserves—in many ways, success or failure in that regard is up to the individual judgment of the reader. But the thing that burned in the pit of my stomach through all of this was the painful awareness of the fact that for hundreds of years, white supremacists have used European mythology and folklore as a tool to excuse or justify their atrocities while systematically destroying or suppressing the mythologies (and languages, and cultures, and lifestyles) of people around the world. When it came right down to it, I really, really didn't want racists to be able to like this book.

So there it is. The two issues—exploitation of the land and of our fellow humans—are deeply interwoven. The harm we have inflicted on our vulnerable communities is reflected in the harm that we are perpetrating on the environment—the ways we strip our land for natural resources, squandering the nonrenewable while neglecting the renewable; the ways we allow corporate interests to prevent environmental regulations to be put in place to prevent further damage; the ways we as a society constantly cite cost as a valid reason for not moving ahead on widespread adoption of green energy, as if money mattered more than people's lives—these, along with ongoing oppression, colonialism, and racism, are all symptoms of the same fundamental rot in the foundation of our society.

And yet. And yet. The beautiful thing about the natural environment is in its infinite ability to adapt and change. Where once many of us were killed, now we survive—though often just barely—and we look towards a future where we can all thrive. What has been done to our land and our people cannot ever be undone and must not be forgotten, but eventually even decay gives way to new growth. Or so we hope, anyway.

If you enjoy this book—and I will be the first to assure you that it barely scratches the surface of the rich and vibrant spectrum of beliefs, folklore, and mythology that the world offers—then I encourage you to seek out the work of marginalized creators, to become a patron of their arts and to uplift and amplify their voices whenever possible.

If you take anything from this book, remember: Sometimes, when you least expect it, you find small wonders flourishing in hidden, forgotten spaces.

Index

About the Author

Alexandra Rowland is the author of *A Conspiracy of Truths*; its sequel, *A Choir of Lies*; and *Finding Faeries*. They are also occasionally a bespoke seamstress under the stern supervision of their feline quality-control manager. They hold a degree in world literature, mythology, and folklore from Truman State University, and they are one of three hosts of the Hugo Award–nominated literary podcast *Be the Serpent*. Find them at AlexandraRowland.net, on Twitter as @_alexrowland, or wandering the woods of western Massachusetts.